"What are you doing?" Kinley asked.

They were so close that the warmth of her breath brushed across his cheek.

The warmth of the sun staring down at them beat against his back. Heat spread through him.

Her mouth was so close. His gaze zeroed in on her lips. The shape of them. The tempting way her upper lip bowed in the center. The tip of her tongue swept out, wetting her bottom lip before disappearing.

He wanted to dive after it. Coax her out with his own tongue. Taste every inch of her gleaming skin.

Jameson waited for her to push him away. To yell at him. Something.

When she didn't, he growled, "To hell with it."

The moment his mouth touched hers, he was lost. All coherent thought fled. The buzz in his blood ramped higher, drowning out every sound and sensation except her.

* * *

Big Easy Secrets by Kira Sinclair
is part of the Bad Billionaires series.

Dear Reader,

Sometimes characters pop onto the page and you just know they deserve their own story. That was the case with Jameson "Joker" Neally when I first started writing the Bad Billionaires series. And when Kinley came along...I knew they'd be perfect for each other—eventually.

So often, we highlight relationships that start with opposites attracting. It's an immediate source of conflict. But what happens when two characters have similarities and somehow still can't keep from clashing? Just because you share an interest, a viewpoint or even some traumatic history doesn't mean that you'll always see eye to eye. Or that things will be easy.

Jameson and Kinley have similar lives and backgrounds. They have interests that should be a source of immediate connection. But they also have very different ways to protect themselves from the trauma they've experienced. Ultimately, those similarities will help bridge the gap between what they think they want and what they really need—each other.

Oh, but the sparks that fly along the way.

I hope you enjoy reading Jameson and Kinley's story. I'd love to hear from you at www.kirasinclair.com, or come chat with me on Twitter @kiraSinclair. And don't forget to check out the other Bad Billionaires!

Best wishes,

Kira

KIRA SINCLAIR

BIG EASY SECRETS

HARLEQUIN
DESIRE

Recycling programs for this product may not exist in your area.

ISBN-13: 978-1-335-58173-0

Big Easy Secrets

Copyright © 2023 by Kira Bazzel

For questions and comments about the quality of this book, please contact us at CustomerService@Harlequin.com.

Harlequin Enterprises ULC
22 Adelaide St. West, 41st Floor
Toronto, Ontario M5H 4E3, Canada
www.Harlequin.com

Printed in U.S.A.

Kira Sinclair's first foray into writing romance was for a high school English assignment, and not even being forced to read the Scotland-set historical aloud to the class could dampen her enthusiasm... although it definitely made her blush. She sold her first book to Harlequin Blaze in 2007 and has enjoyed exploring relationships, falling in love and happily-ever-afters since. She lives in North Alabama with her two teenage daughters and their ever-entertaining bernedoodle puppy, Sadie. Kira loves to hear from readers at Kira@KiraSinclair.com.

Books by Kira Sinclair

Harlequin Desire

Bad Billionaires

The Rebel's Redemption
The Devil's Bargain
The Sinner's Secret
Secrets, Vegas Style
Blame It on Vegas
Big Easy Secrets

Visit the Author Profile page
at Harlequin.com for more titles.

You can also find Kira Sinclair on Facebook,
along with other Harlequin Desire authors,
at Facebook.com/harlequindesireauthors!

I'd like to dedicate this book to
Tressie Mullins and all my friends
at The Compound. We sweat together,
grind together, curse the heat and laugh.
You help keep me going just when I need
a push and provide a safe space to just be me.
My life is much richer because you're in it.
Thank you for all you do!

One

Son of a... Kinley Sullivan stared at the zeros blinking on the screen. *No, this can't be right.*

As much as she wanted this to be a nightmare, the cool rush of air across her skin and the hollow, churning sensation in her belly told her it wasn't.

She was flat broke. It was gone. All of it. Almost fifty million dollars just...gone.

What was worse, someone had turned the tables. Used her own methods to steal from her. The betrayal and sense of violation made her feel sick. The fact that every cent she had was gone meant not only that she was in a hell of a lot of trouble, but that she had zero resources to fight whatever was coming next.

Her past was finally catching up to her.

Dammit, she thought she'd have more time. More time to do good. More time to make amends.

Kinley had always known eventually someone she'd pissed off would find her. You can't steal money from the powerful and depraved—not to mention criminal—without stirring up a giant need for revenge. She supposed, considering she'd been doing this for almost twelve years—since she was sixteen—that she'd had a good run.

Unfortunately, whoever had found her most likely wouldn't be happy just to have their money back. No, they'd want a pound of flesh as well. And if they'd found her private accounts, they could no doubt find *her*.

That thought sent Kinley vaulting up from her chair. The casters rattled as they rolled across the hardwood floor of the penthouse she'd been occupying for the past three months. With a sigh, she raced into her bedroom and grabbed the go bag she always had prepared.

After the incident with her half brother and the Russian mob a year ago- the first time she'd come face-to-face with the half brother she hadn't known existed until she was sixteen- she'd come to realize that at some point she'd have to leave her equipment behind.

That day had apparently come.

Snatching up the flash drive disguised as a silver pendant, Kinley looped it over her head. The cool metal settled beneath her T-shirt in the valley between her breasts. She had no idea what she would do with it, but the incriminating evidence was too important to abandon with everything else.

Stuffing the one laptop she'd grabbed into her worn backpack, the telltale sound of an email dropping into her inbox stalled her momentum.

Opening the lid, she quickly scanned the notification on her screen. The lines of the email were completely blank, which was unusual as hell. No To, Subject, anything.

Kinley's heart fluttering as she double clicked.

And let out a long string of curses when the message opened.

She was going to kill the bastard.

Jameson Neally, aka Joker, settled into the welcoming comfort of the custom computer chair. It had cost him a fortune, but considering he spent close to sixteen hours a day in front of a computer, money well spent. And he could afford it so…

The room around him was dark, broken only by the glow of multiple computer screens. It was late, but it wouldn't have mattered if it was high noon. No light reached into the basement where he'd set up his workspace. And that was just how he liked it. Not because he had a problem with sunlight, but because he had a problem with nosy neighbors and prying eyes.

For the most part, he kept to himself. But on the few occasions he'd spoken to the couple next door or the elderly woman who lived with her four cats across the street, he'd been polite, and vague about what he did for a living.

Because the homeowners' association might take exception to a hacker freelancing out of his basement. The neighborhood was upper middle class. Cookie-cutter houses that cost more than they should and provided less space between each structure than anyone liked. Normal.

And he'd made it his. Home.

He'd bought the place several years ago so that he could blend in, but realized he actually liked it. The neighborhood reminded him of the one he and his parents had lived in together...until they'd died and he was left utterly alone.

Tampa gave him sun year-round, even if he didn't get to enjoy it very often. It was a big city, somewhere he could disappear into the backdrop if he needed to.

But none of that particularly mattered right now. In between his other jobs, he'd spent the past year monitoring one woman. Not because he was being paid to—although he was—but because he couldn't have stopped if he'd wanted to.

Kinley Sullivan fascinated him and had from the first moment she'd popped onto his computer screen. She was brilliant, resourceful. And a loner just like him.

Despite never meeting in person, they had a...complicated history.

Dropping his head against the rest, Joker squeezed his eyes shut and sighed. No doubt, Kinley Sullivan would kill him for what he'd just done. But at least no one would be killing her. Tonight. Assuming she used the plane ticket he'd just emailed her.

Sure, she'd be pissed that he'd stolen all her money, but that was what happened when you refused to engage for over a year and some really bad guys finally caught up with you.

Joker wasn't even sure who the bad guys were, but it didn't matter. Kinley had a way of pissing off very powerful and ruthless people. He could figure out who the threat was—this time—when she showed up on his doorstep.

Please let her show up on his doorstep.

If Gray Lockwood, Kinley's half brother and Joker's friend and sometimes boss, found out what he'd done… The man definitely wouldn't appreciate Joker's methods. Although it wasn't like he'd had much choice. Joker had been tracking Kinley for months and she was always a step ahead of him.

Which was frustrating and humbling. Especially considering that the last time they had found her she was being shot at by the Russian mob. Danger had a way of finding Kinley Sullivan and for some reason, Joker had this undying urge to protect her.

Mostly from herself.

She was alone, and had been for so long. But there were people out there who wanted to help her. Gray had told him not to push. To just watch. Gray wanted Kinley to come in out of the cold of her own choice.

Joker understood Gray's reasoning. Kinley needed to decide that she wanted to trust them. Gray also understood the resentment that came with losing your freedom and choices. He'd spent ten years in prison for a crime he didn't commit.

And complicating the entire situation was that Kinley had been the one to frame him for that crime. Sure, she hadn't realized what she was doing or who she was setting up at the time, but…

Complications.

Which was why they'd simply been watching and waiting. Until tonight.

Gray might not agree with Joker's plan, but it was too late now. Kinley's money was gone, sitting in one of his own offshore accounts. No reason to get Gray involved. Yet. Not until she actually showed up and he figured out just how much trouble she was in.

"You asshole."

Joker whipped his head around at the sound of a smoky voice. His heart leaped into his chest, even as his brain registered exactly who'd walked into his private sanctuary. Hours before the plane ticket he'd sent her yesterday should have had her landing.

How the hell had she found him? And how had she gotten into his basement without tripping any of the state-of-the-art alarms set up around his perimeter?

The thump of his heartbeat had nothing to do with fear. Well, not true fear as he didn't think Kinley had a bloodthirsty bone in her body. Even so, his plan for their first meeting had involved a crowded coffee shop in the hopes of using the cover of innocent people to mitigate her anger while he convinced her that he hadn't actually screwed her over. Neither of them wanted to draw attention to themselves so an audience meant no shouting.

Obviously, that plan hadn't panned out.

Bright blue eyes, the color of a clear summer sky, flashed with pure, unadulterated fury as Kinley stomped across the wide expanse of his basement. The fingers of her right hand curled around the butt of a dark gray gun as she advanced on him.

Maybe he needed more field time if the first thing he noticed was the color of her eyes and not the gun pointed at his chest. And perhaps he didn't know her as well as he thought he did after eleven months, twenty-one days and sixteen hours of surveillance.

Not that he'd been counting.

The basement spread the entire length of the house, one solid room set up with banks of servers, cooling equipment, monitors, keyboards and wires. Above, his home was unassuming in every possible way. He worked hard to maintain the front of a reclusive, slightly nerdy IT guy.

And, of course, part of that facade was accurate.

Jameson's eyes narrowed as his calculating gaze measured Kinley's intent. His body tensed, preparing to respond in whatever way he needed. Preferably, in a way that would cause a minimal amount of damage to the woman he was currently trying to protect.

The gun remained unwavering as she slowly advanced forward, but judging by her body language, he didn't think she'd really pull the trigger. No one who spent their lives stealing from drug dealers and donating the money to drug rehab programs could really kill someone, right?

"Where's my money?" The bite of her words stung him.

Rising slowly from the chair, Joker held his hands

up in the universal sign for peace and innocence. "Why don't you put the gun down, Kinley?"

"Why don't you give my money back, Jameson?"

Of course she knew his real name. Only a handful of people did, including his handler at the FBI, her brother and his partners at Stone Surveillance, and the only friend from his childhood that he kept in touch with. He shouldn't be surprised, but he was.

"I will."

The harsh sound of her skepticism scraped through her throat, but he had to admit to a little spurt of relief when the gun lowered to point at the ground.

"I swear, Kinley. I just needed to get you to come in. That's all."

Her mouth twisted into a grimace. "And you didn't think to simply ask?"

This time, it was his turn to issue a disbelieving sound. "Please. I've been asking for almost a year and you've been ignoring me."

"Maybe you should take the hint. Or ask a little nicer."

Jameson took several slow steps forward. Kinley didn't flinch or let herself be cowed by his advance. "Or maybe I needed to back you into a corner. Kinley, you're in danger."

A single eyebrow rose over those mesmerizing eyes. "So what's new? I've pissed off a lot of bad guys. Gray let me go last time. I've always wondered why. I knew you were his bulldog. Watching and waiting until he was ready to take his pound of flesh?"

Her harsh words hurt, not because she'd called him a bulldog, but because she'd been so screwed over for so long—by everyone in her life—that it was clear she simply expected the worst from everyone.

He'd watched her for months. Knew she let no one in. She didn't have any friends. Hell, she didn't even have acquaintances. Or a goldfish.

One loner recognized another.

She really did have everything twisted inside her head.

"Gray has no idea what's going on here. And this is more than your regular danger. This isn't some angry South American drug lord or Eastern European arms dealer. Those people are easy to identify, and counter surveil. I don't know who you've pissed off this time," Which scared the hell out of him. "But they meant business. And they were closing in fast. I knew you wouldn't listen to reason."

A muscle in her jaw twitched and her fingers tightened around the butt of the gun. "And you thought cornering me, leaving me with absolutely no resources, was the best way to get what you wanted?"

Jameson shrugged and couldn't help the smug smile that played across his lips. "You're here, aren't you?"

Slowly, the gun rose between them again. Faint light from the screens behind him flickered across her face. Joker didn't follow the track of the gun, but kept his gaze focused solely on her eyes. He watched for her intent even as the dark, gaping hole at the end of the pistol trained on center mass.

Everything sharpened. The slightly musty scent that pervaded the basement no matter how much he tried to combat it. The hot, metallic overtones from the machines surrounding them. The hum of electronics and the buzz of multiple cooling fans. The whiff of her perfume, something subtle and floral, sweet. The flutter of her dark hair as it swirled around her shoulders, tickling the sharp cheekbones that slashed across her aristocratic face.

He saw the conflict warring inside her. Part of her wanted to hurt him, and he honestly didn't blame her, but she wouldn't.

Kinley Sullivan had been on the run since she was sixteen. Alone, with no one to depend on or trust. Hell, she'd been that way long before she'd run away from her parents and the criminal life they'd built in Vegas.

"Look, I'll show you the accounts if it'll make you feel better. Tell me where you want me to send the money and I'll give it all back. I have no intention of taking what's yours, Kinley. I just want to help. Want to make sure you're safe."

The gun pointing at his chest didn't move, but her head tilted slightly to the side.

Jameson pushed his luck by adding, "so does your brother."

"Yeah, right. I ruined his life."

He understood why she might think she had, but the reality was a heck of a lot more complicated than that. "You didn't, but that's a conversation between you and him."

"And the minute I put away this gun you're going to leap across this room, lock me down and take me to him, aren't you?"

The level of distrust in her voice saddened him.

"No. If Gray had wanted you forcibly brought to him, he could have done that months ago."

"Yeah, right." This time it was her lips that quirked up into a knowing grin. "We both know you've been chasing me for almost a year, always a day late and a dollar short."

She wasn't wrong. And, sure, it stung just a little. But that truth also intrigued him. More than he wanted to admit.

He was damn good at his job. But in the dark recesses of his own mind, he could admit that she was better. Not that he'd ever voice those words aloud. Not even with her gun held straight to his head.

"Either way, you have my word. This has nothing to do with Gray. You were in danger, and forcing your hand was the only way I could think to keep you safe."

Slowly, Joker twisted toward a keyboard. With a single finger, he tapped on several keys until the information he wanted scrolled across the screen behind him. From his precarious position, he couldn't see the entire screen, but he was confident at what would be there.

Until she said, "I don't find that very funny, Joker. I've already seen my bank account and the copious zeros that now reside there."

What was she talking about? Whipping his head around, Joker stared at the screen. Where millions of dollars should have sat, now only three zeros and a single decimal point blinked at him.

"Son of a…"

Some else was one step ahead of them both.

Two

She wanted to scream. But she couldn't afford to let the man in front of her see the frustration and fear running rampant through her system.

She was dead broke.

The familiar anxiety that she'd fought for the first couple years she'd been alone punched through her gut. It had been a long time since she'd felt so helpless. Sure, she'd had millions of dollars in her account, but touching that money had made her feel guilty since it was stolen. Still, she'd been sixteen and a runaway, fending for herself. Hiding from people who wanted to harm her.

The danger had always been there, lurking around every corner. It had taken her a little while to decide that since she already had a target on her back, and the skills to make others pay for their crimes, she might as well use her powers for good. The more criminals she'd stolen from, the more enemies she gained.

At some point, she became numb to it.

But yesterday, Jameson Neally had stolen her safety net. It had been a long time since she'd felt that…helpless. God, she wanted to hurt him. But that wasn't the kind of person she was.

Would never be the kind of person she'd let herself become. Even if that was what her parents had raised her to be.

Gritting her teeth, Kinley ground out, "Exactly where is my money?"

The *oh shit* expression on Joker's face told her everything she needed to know. But a tiny kernel deep inside hoped he was just messing with her.

"Uh…"

"You lost it?"

Shaking his head, Joker leaned over the keyboard and started pounding furiously on the keys. The dark strands of his long shaggy hair fell to shield his face.

Oh no, she wanted to see his expression.

Before she even realized what she was doing, Kinley reached over and tucked the sleek strands behind his ear. Her own eyes widened, not just at the jolt of something that shot up her fingers, but at the fact that she'd touched him at all.

For all she'd been studying him, tracking him, watching him… Jameson Neally was a stranger.

Joker was so engrossed in what he was doing, he didn't even seem to notice she'd touched him. Which would have been slightly demoralizing if she let herself care.

The strong features of his face pulled tight with concentration. His lips, framed by his well-manicured beard, thinned. Clearly, the man was frustrated.

"Lost?" she asked again, the single word sticking in her throat.

"Stolen." Ripping the dark-rimmed glasses from his face, Joker flung them onto the desk. They skittered across the slick surface and stopped just before teetering over the edge. Strong, hard fingers tugged at the messy mop of hair curling into his eyes. Sweeping it back, he jerked it tight enough to tug at the edges of his temples as he wrapped a band around it to tie it out of the way.

Something told her this was a movement he didn't even realize he was making. Pure habit.

"Stolen." Of course her money had been stolen from the thief who'd taken it from her. Because that's how her life went.

Nothing could be easy. Oh, no, not for her.

"Who took it? And how do you propose we get it back?" Because really, that was all she cared about. That money kept her safe. Provided her resources and protection from the bad guys she'd been hunting for so long. Sure, she could steal more, but that would defeat the purpose of her life's work.

She never kept any of the money she took, because it was destined for more important purposes. The money Joker had taken was the seed money that she'd stolen from Lockwood Industries, her brother's family company. The money that Gray had been wrongly convicted of embezzling. Yes, she'd used some in the beginning, but only what she'd needed to survive. And over the years, she'd made sure to replace what she'd taken. Now she only dipped into it when absolutely necessary. Because the money wasn't really hers.

Every day of her life, until she was sixteen, had been a lie. A perfectly crafted one, but a lie nonetheless. She'd been born to two criminals, raised to be just like them. She'd been...probably eleven or twelve before she realized the things her parents had her do weren't normal.

Breaking into buildings. Scamming people. Stealing. Using the skills her father had carefully taught her in order to hack in and take what they wanted.

Not what *she* wanted, but what *they* wanted.

All she'd wanted was to be a normal teenager. Get grounded for staying out past curfew. Have the keys taken away when she sneaked out to some party and had a couple drinks. But no, she'd been the teenager dressing like a celebrity socialite and pretending to be the queen bee to scam money from the high-rolling millionaires who'd come to Vegas for some fun.

The bright lights and big city had been a hunting ground for her parents. For her, it had been a prison. One she plotted and finally escaped.

At the expense of the half brother she didn't even know existed. The theft had been carefully crafted by her mother to finally make her ex-husband, Gray's father, pay for tossing her away. But in double crossing her parents, Kinley had framed the wrong man. Gray had been convicted of embezzlement and sentenced to ten years in prison.

Guilt mixed with anxiety, a toxic combination bubbling just beneath her skin. She needed that money.

"There is no we. I lost it, so I'll find it."

A harsh sound came from Kinley's throat. "Excuse me if I don't trust the man who took everything from me. I'm not letting you out of my sight until I have all my money back. Every single penny."

For the first time since he'd pulled up the bank account, Joker—no, Jameson—looked at her. Really looked.

His soft green eyes sharpened. Kinley already knew the man was brilliant. While he'd been watching her for the past year, she'd been surveilling him. Learning as much as she possible could about her brother's watchdog.

Joker was notorious as a hacker. He had a reputation for being perfect. He was very choosy about the jobs he accepted and absolutely never failed. He'd also built a swirl of mystery around himself. Very few people knew much of anything about the actual man.

He was a myth. A legend.

And something told her that wasn't an accident or simply fate. Jameson Neally had worked hard to build this persona.

The man in front of her didn't quite fit what she'd expected. He was gorgeous in an unkempt, distracted sort of way. His body wasn't soft from hours sitting in front of a computer and eating nothing but chips and French fries. No, beneath the tight Henley and worn jeans the man had a killer body.

Not that she was looking. Or cared.

But since he'd carefully cultivated a reputation for excellence, the fact that he was staring at her now with sorrow and guilt in his eyes...scared the hell out of her.

"I have no idea where it is, Kinley, but I promise I'm going to find it. Truly, my intention was to protect you. Help you."

"Clearly, that backfired."

"Clearly."

Yanking his hands through his hair, Jameson undid the knot he'd tied before tying it again. Definitely a habit. "Look, I feel like shit about this."

"You should."

His eyes closed and his head tilted as a groan rumbled through his throat. Kinley tried hard not to notice the long, strong column or the way the muscles in his neck worked on the sound.

Seriously, what was wrong with her? This guy had stolen from her, manipulated her and lost everything that she had.

Closing the gap between them, he reached for her. Kinley's instinct was to flinch, but she refused to give in to the ingrained response. Without a doubt, she knew Jameson Neally would never physically hurt her.

"I'm going to find the money, Kinley. I promise."

"I don't need your help. I can find it myself. Send me all the info that you have."

"No."

Kinley shook her head. Maybe she'd heard him wrong. "What do you mean, no?"

"No, I can't do that. Don't get me wrong, this situation sucks, but the danger that started this whole thing is real and those people are still hot on your trail."

And now she had no resources to run. "And you've left me with nothing."

A chagrined expression crossed his face.

"I don't trust you, Joker."

"You don't trust anyone, Kinley."

He wasn't wrong, but that was beside the point. "You've caused enough trouble. Give me the info and I'll be out of your hair."

"Not happening."

Clearly, the hardheaded man wasn't going to budge.

"Fine." Spinning on her heel, Kinley headed for the door. "I'll take care of this on my own." Stopping in the doorway, she paused to turn and look at him. "You're an asshole."

She wasn't wrong, but that wasn't going to stop him from doing what he needed in order to protect her.

Narrowing his eyes, Joker calculated the odds and realized it was time to pull out the ace up his sleeve.

"You walk out that door and I'll call your brother. He'll have a team of people tracking you within ten minutes of leaving here."

Jameson watched Kinley's face blanch of all color. And he hated himself for causing that kind of reaction in her. He didn't need a psychology degree to understand her response. Given their history, it was clear Kinley assumed her brother had nothing but ill will toward her. Which he knew for a fact wasn't the case.

Gray Lockwood only wanted to protect his sister. Which was why Joker had been watching her in the first place. But his friend had also given him strict instructions not to force Kinley's hand. Gray wanted her to come to him when she felt ready. Safe.

After watching her for months, Joker was of the opinion Kinley would never get to that point unless something pushed her. And while that hadn't been his intention with his actions, it might end up being a happy side effect.

"Why? Why would you do that when you know I don't want to see him?"

And there it was, confirmation that he was right. And even though she wouldn't believe him, he'd say it to her again. "Because your brother worries about you, Kinley."

"Bullshit."

Joker simply shook his head. No words would convince her. The guilt she felt every time Gray's name was mentioned was so clear that she might as well have taken out a billboard to display it.

Jameson gave in to the sigh he'd been holding back. He heard the hope and disappointment in Gray's voice each time he mentioned Kinley, even if his friend tried to hide it. He could see the evidence of Kinley's fear, guilt and hunger for something she didn't think she could have. It sucked being stuck in the middle. "Look, I get this is a crappy situation."

Kinley's short and pointed words hit their mark. "That you caused."

"Fine, that I caused." He had no problems admitting the truth, although he wouldn't have changed anything. "We have a better shot at recovering your money if we work together. You have to admit that."

Kinley opened her mouth to argue; he could see that clearly in the stubborn set of her jaw and the tight tilt of her shoulders. But something stopped her. Several seconds passed, one beat and then two more. Finally, she said, "I can agree with that much."

Well, it was a step in the right direction. He'd take it.

"I know you don't want to get Gray involved." He held up a hand to stop her argument. "I don't need to understand why. Your relationship with him is complicated. I promise not to tell him you're here, with me, if you agree to work together. Once we have your money back, you can go on your merry way."

"Gee, thanks for permission, Dad." No doubt, she'd meant the sarcasm to cut, but in reality Jameson had to force down a laugh.

"You're in danger, Kinley. If you don't want Gray's help, at least accept mine."

Her face scrunched up and her teeth ground together. "You really haven't given me much choice, have you? All of my resources are gone. I have only the things I was able to grab from my place and pack into my single suitcase."

Sweeping his arms around, Jameson indicated the

huge expanse of his basement and all the equipment. "What's mine is yours."

He watched the war as her brain fought, practicality against fear. Thank God, practicality won.

"Fine. At least for now."

Snatching up the glasses he'd thrown onto the table, Jameson said, "Great. First things first, who the hell have you pissed off?"

Kinley crooked an eyebrow. "The better question to ask is who haven't I pissed off."

Wonderful, that was exactly what he was afraid of. "We know you've been compromised and considering someone just stole all your money out of my secure accounts, we can assume I have been, too. I have a safe house set up, so I suggest we spend the next couple hours packing up so we can hightail it out of here."

As much as Kinley was a loner, so was he. But while she moved around every few months, Jameson had worked hard to build a home base that he loved. His house in the suburbs of Tampa was the perfect setup, in a good neighborhood with neighbors who left him alone. He knew the people close to him, at the local coffee shop and bakery. But while they were acquaintances, he'd always been careful not to leave crumbs that led back to who he really was or what he really did.

After the upheaval of his childhood, it had been important to him to plant some roots, even if they'd only been superficial ones. Walking away from his home, even for a little while, irritated him. But it was necessary.

And at least he had a luxurious alternative waiting for him. One he loved just as much.

"Fine, but I'm only agreeing to stick around for a couple days. Until I get a better idea of what's going on and can regroup."

No doubt by then she'd be able to scrounge up some resources and run. Again. Or, at least that was probably what she was planning.

Good thing he had another ace up his sleeve, one that would keep her absolutely safe.

Even if it would piss her off all over again.

Okay, this was not what she'd expected.

Kinley might have spent most of her adult life overseas, but she tracked many of the rich, famous and morally corrupt, so she was familiar enough with the Florida lifestyle. Miami, Palm Beach, the Keys. She'd never visited before now, though. Most of the time her job didn't require physical access to people or places. She could work from afar to topple criminals.

When Jameson told her that he had a safe house, never in a million years did she expect to be standing at one of the most exclusive yacht harbors in the city. Staring up at a monstrosity of a yacht.

Realizing her mouth was hanging open, Kinley snapped it shut.

Her bank account might have had plenty of zeros, but she only played on the edges of the rich and famous. She didn't spend that money on herself and never had a drive to. Not after watching her parents build a life of wealth and affluence based solely on lying, cheating and stealing.

None of the material trappings that society viewed as evidence of success mattered to her.

Apparently, they mattered to Joker, which only confirmed her opinion of him. The man had a wonky moral compass. He might be picky about his clients, but that didn't mean he refused to accept jobs that were closer to black than gray on the morality scale.

Mega yachts lined both sides of a pier. An ostentatious display of wealth. Joker strode past her without pausing, heading straight for the yacht directly in front of them. He approached a group of people clustered on the jetty and greeted them with a smile before turning to her.

"Kinley, this is our captain, Eric."

The smartly dressed man gave her a small wave. "Welcome aboard. The staff and I will take great care of you."

Kinley blinked. Of course there was a staff. "Uh, thanks."

Eric introduced the others standing behind him. Frank, second in command, Rachel, the chef, and Meg, housekeeping and hospitality. Did they really need four people to take care of them for the few days they might be gone?

Blinking, Kinley decided she had no idea how many people it took to keep the monstrosity in front of her operational and afloat. Which was something that clearly needed to happen. Unexpected trepidation rolled through her belly. She'd never been on so much as a fishing charter, let alone a yacht. What if she got seasick?

Turning to Joker, she said, "I don't know about this."

A cocky grin curled the edges of his lips. "Trust me, it will be fine."

Easy for him to say.

Wrapping his arm around her shoulders, Joker began to gently, purposefully urge her closer to the ship. She wanted to dig her feet into the solid ground beneath her, but for some reason her body wouldn't obey the command. The name of the ship—*Queen of Hearts*—flashed by as they moved up the gangway and onto the deck.

And the entire world didn't pitch sideways beneath her feet.

Okay, maybe this wasn't so bad.

Twisting, Kinley looked behind her to find the crew scurrying as they loaded their bags and what looked like boxes of supplies.

Rachel appeared in front of her; how had that happened? She could have sworn the woman was still on the dock. Holding out a glass filled with frosty pink liquid, she said, "Enjoy."

Instinct had Kinley grasping it and Joker's urging had her taking a sip. Strawberry daiquiri. Holding it away from her, Kinley said, "Isn't it a little early to be drinking?"

A wide grin stretched across Jameson's lips. The merry twinkle in his pale green eyes changed the entire demeanor of his face. Gone was the cerebral, slightly nerdy guy, replaced by a mischievous devil who enjoyed convincing others to sin.

Kinley blinked, slightly surprised by the transformation, but had to admit both sides of Jameson's personality were smoking hot. Damn him.

Walking her through the ship, Joker gave her the abbreviated tour. Staterooms, living area, galley, entertainment space, bar, water closets. Ten minutes from the time they'd boarded, Kinley found herself standing on the open deck, staring out across the large expanse of crystal-blue water while Tampa disappeared into the distance.

Her head spun, not from the motion of the yacht, but from the speed with which her life had just moved completely out of her control. It was a sensation she did not like. It had been a long time—twelve years to be exact—since anyone had made decisions for her.

Irritation finally surfaced. Even as she looked out over the complete luxury that surrounded her, realization dawned. The *Queen of Hearts* was a beautiful, gilded cage. Complete with state-of-the-art electronics, a hot tub and a plunge pool open to the sunshine and stars. Plush couches and chairs and comfortable loungers and hammocks.

Taking a gulp of her drink, she decided it probably wasn't too early to indulge after all.

"You own this." It wasn't a question. The staff knew him and from the way they'd greeted Jameson, were quite friendly with him. Sure, it was possible he'd simply cultivated a friendship with the crew and they allowed him to use their boss's yacht when it wasn't in use. But she hadn't gotten that impression.

"Yes."

Slowly, Kinley looked around. "How much?"

"What?"

"How much is this yacht worth?"

He had the foresight to look slightly chagrined. "A few million."

Clearly. "Exactly how few?"

Joker lifted his own glass filled with something clear and sparkly and mumbled behind it.

"I'm sorry, what did you say?"

With a sigh, he lowered the glass and enunciated the words. "Twenty-six million."

Holy shit. It wasn't that the number itself overwhelmed her. Hell, her own bank account had held almost twice that. It was the idea that he'd spent that much on something that extravagant. She knew he had money, but if his toy cost this much…

Rolling his eyes, Joker said, "Oh, don't look at me like that."

"Like what?"

"Like I'm some villain in a bad movie. Yes, I've made my share of money."

It was Kinley's turn to hide her words behind her glass. "By stealing, hacking and helping criminals."

But apparently, he heard her. "I admit in my early years, I took some jobs I'm not proud of. And profited. But that was a long time ago and I've spent years trying to make up for that." His gaze was pointed as he added, "Something I'd think you'd be familiar with. Atoning for mistakes."

She couldn't quite stop the wince. "That doesn't make keeping the results of your ill-gotten gains right."

The wicked grin that curled across his lips sent little sparks of something rampaging through her belly. "It doesn't make it wrong, either. Trust me, I'm not that person anymore."

Trust him. Ha! Setting her glass on the nearby table, she turned to face him. "I don't want or need to trust you, Joker."

Leaning forward, Jameson invaded her personal space to place his glass next to hers. Kinley sucked in a surprised breath as the warmth from his body melted against her skin and the tempting scent of him bombarded her senses.

Pulling back, he stared at her with those pale green eyes. "Admit it, you and I aren't that different."

Kinley scoffed, the noise scraping through her throat. "Please, just because we're both hackers doesn't make us the same. I steal from terrible people and use the money I take to right the wrongs they've inflicted on the world. From where I'm standing—" her pointed gaze took in their luxurious surroundings "—we're nothing alike."

A small smile tugged at the corners of Jameson's lips, but something dark and sad filled his eyes. "It must be so lonely up there in your ivory tower. Perfect and superior."

It was. The thought was through her head before

she'd even really had it. Her life was lonely and had been for a very long time. But it was her life, and she'd come to accept that as the price she paid to look herself in the mirror at night. What she did was dangerous and she couldn't justify placing anyone else's life in jeopardy.

But she wasn't about to admit that to him.

So instead, she focused on his other statement. "I don't think I'm perfect or superior." He made her sound like some stuck-up snob on a personal crusade.

Jameson's pointed response, a single quirked eyebrow, left her no room to continue protesting. Not without appearing desperate to correct his opinion of her.

Which she wasn't. She didn't care what he thought. Seriously, she didn't.

Her mouth tightened, an attempt to keep the words that wanted to spill out contained behind her teeth.

A knowing smirk spread slowly across Jameson's wide mouth. "If you say so."

God, she wanted to wipe that expression right off his face.

But his next words stopped her.

"You want to see my server room?"

Kinley slowly blinked. Her chest was tight with irritation. A huge part of her wanted to turn around and walk away. But he'd tantalized her with the one carrot she couldn't refuse.

Damn him.

Three

When Jameson fantasized about Kinley drooling over his equipment, he hadn't exactly envisioned her starry eyes would be for the computers on his yacht. Standing in the doorway, she stared at his setup like most women might look at chocolate-covered strawberries or crème brûlée.

But there was no way he was letting her get her hands on his equipment.

Not only did his system contain sensitive information about jobs that he'd worked, but it also held info he needed to keep compartmentalized and protected.

Along with Stone Surveillance, he worked to help domestic violence victims disappear by providing them new identities and monitoring their previous abusers to ensure safety. While he didn't expect Kinley would do anything to jeopardize those men and women, he'd made them and Gray a promise of secrecy and he meant to keep it.

Not to mention, his system held classified information for the cases he consulted on with the FBI, the CIA and Homeland Security.

All perfectly good reasons to deny her access. But he was also afraid that if Kinley did get in, she'd find some way to send out a bat signal, hack a drug lord or plant herself a back door into his files so she could wreak havoc and get revenge for what had happened.

Or more likely all three.

Leaning out into the hallway, Jameson signaled to Rachel. His staff were impeccable, not just because they were damn good at their jobs, but because every last one of them knew what he needed with little more than a look and a gesture.

He kept the crew on retainer, although they also held other positions in the area. Luckily most of the team had been able to sail with short notice.

A bright smile on her face, Rachel swept into the room, hooked an arm through Kinley's and began urging her out toward the stairs leading to the main deck. "Why don't we discuss your food preferences while you're on board. Any allergies?"

"No." Kinley barely acknowledged Rachel's jabber and questions. Her neck swiveled so that she could stare at the bank of expensive computers, terminals and servers they left behind. Like a toddler gazing longingly at the toy her mother wouldn't buy her.

"I'll fix you another drink and we already have

snacks by the pool. The warm breeze is nice today, right?"

Jameson watched as they moved out of range. Kinley's eyes cleared, almost as if the hypnotizing charm of his equipment had been broken once she couldn't see it anymore. Her eyebrows beetled. "Shouldn't you have asked me my preferences and allergies before loading all the supplies onto the ship and pushing away from dry land?"

Rachel's laugh was a little brittle. "Oh, we have lots of options. And Mr. Neally supplied us with some basic information. I just wanted to make sure we hadn't missed anything."

The two women veered off in one direction while he used the distraction Rachel provided to disappear in the opposite.

Pausing in one of the crew rooms, he pulled out the phone that had been slipped from Kinley's baggage. Making quick work of it, he cloned her cell so that he would get a copy of every email, text message or notification she received.

That accomplished, he headed out to find one of Rachel's team so they could replace the phone in Kinley's luggage before she realized it was missing. Then he hunted down the captain.

It didn't take him long to find Eric issuing orders to the rest of his crew. Normally, the yacht employed a larger staff, but for obvious reasons he'd requested that Eric, Frank, Rachel and Meg work with a skeleton crew. There were another three on board, although he was still paying the crew who hadn't come on this trip. The fewer people aware of Kinley's presence, the better. Loose lips and ships and everything.

Jameson waited until Eric was finished before asking to speak with him. Gesturing, he led his friend into a quiet, private corner.

"I need you to do me a favor."

"Whatever you need."

"I want you to head towards New Orleans. Take us out into open water, but stay close enough that we can get into port within a few hours if necessary. Far enough out that Kinley won't be able to see land."

Eric's eyebrows rose, but he didn't voice the obvious questions that he had. Instead, he simply nodded his agreement.

That hadn't been the difficult part of his request.

"And then I want you to pretend we've had a mechanical failure and we're stuck. I don't care how you sell it, that's up to you. But I want Kinley to think we can't go anywhere for at least a few days."

Eric's head tilted and a knowing grin tugged at his lips. "Do I want to know why?"

Jameson's own mouth twitched. "Probably not."

Shaking his head, Eric's dark, intelligent eyes narrowed. "Who's in trouble, you or her?"

He'd always known the man was sharp, and considering Anderson Stone, the CEO of Stone Surveillance, had recommended him, he wasn't surprised at the easy way Eric rolled with the punches. Or jumped to accurate assumptions.

"Let's just say a little bit of both. However, I don't

trust Kinley to be smart and stay under my protection if she gets a whiff of land."

Especially if they came across any actionable intel.

Jameson had never brought anyone on board the *Queen*, not friends, not business acquaintances and certainly never the handful of women he'd dated. The ship was his oasis, escape and safety net. Which was why he'd only suggested it as a last resort when it had become clear they needed someplace safe to regroup, analyze and do a little cyber digging.

But once he'd thought it through, having Kinley stranded and incapable of escape did provide an added layer of protection. And might allow him to get some actual sleep at night considering he wouldn't need to be on constant watch for her to disappear at the first opportunity.

She might have agreed to work with him, but he wasn't naive. Kinley had been pushed into a corner and the minute she found a way to wiggle free she'd disappear.

Because that's all she'd known since she fled from her parents at sixteen.

She'd agreed to work with him, but he hadn't made the same promise. And when she realized he had no intention of giving her access to anything useful… She was going to be pissed.

Offering a tip of his finger to his forehead, Eric said, "Whatever you need. Let me go inform my crew of our destination."

"Just make sure they're all aware of the ruse, because Kinley is crafty." And with nothing to keep her occupied, she'd no doubt get bored and start poking around because she could.

Jameson watched his captain walk away. He stared down the hallway, surrounded by luxurious furnishings, elegant lighting and all the trappings of wealth. He'd worked hard to earn the *Queen* and had bought her early in his career.

Admittedly, before his moral compass had swung a little closer to the angel side than the devil. Normally, the ship made him feel relaxed and comfortable.

But not today. And that could only be attributed to the woman waiting somewhere above.

He might as well get this over with. On a sigh, he headed up to find her…and no doubt get an earful over something.

Kinley stared out across the deck. Most people, surrounded by luxury, would allow themselves to relax and enjoy. But she couldn't do that. Energy and nerves pulsed through her system.

The note that had been in her mailbox just before she'd left for Tampa hadn't helped. An anonymous demand for the return of the money she'd stolen.

It wasn't the first time she'd been threatened. And it probably wouldn't be the last. Although it did give her pause that whoever had sent it used an address that should have been impossible to find.

For the briefest moment, she thought about sharing the note with Joker, but decided against it.

She wanted to do something. Needed to do something.

But each time she tried to leave the outdoor lounge area one of the staff appeared to block her. Oh, they did it politely, but it was patently clear that she was being purposely kept in one place.

Joker didn't trust her. She supposed she didn't blame him. Kinley didn't trust him, either.

"Standing here, watching the horizon, where the blue sky and turquoise water meet, always gets me."

She hadn't even heard him approach. For a man who spent most of his time in front of a computer, he moved with the grace and stealth of a ninja.

Kinley studied him, letting her gaze travel slowly down his body before going back up again.

Jameson quirked an eyebrow but didn't comment on her calculated perusal. His body didn't tense. He didn't fidget or fuss, but simply stood and let her look.

Something told her there was much more to the man standing beside her than what was visible on the surface. He presented a specific image, but she'd gotten a few glimpses that suggested there was more to the man than he liked people to see.

Which both intrigued and irritated her. Because while that reality told her she couldn't trust the man, something else deep inside her *wanted* to. Which was not smart.

"How often do you get to sail her?" If they were stuck together, she might as well ask some questions. When this was all over, things would return to normal and they'd be back to playing cat and mouse. Having some new intel might prove beneficial.

"Not enough."

"What a generic answer." Shifting, Kinley pressed her back against the polished railing. Better position to watch him. "I expected more from you."

A half smile tugged at his generous lips as he shrugged. "It might be generic, but it's also true."

"You stay that busy, huh?"

"What can I say? Your brother is very persuasive when he wants something. Stone Surveillance has been quietly building a reputation and a client list of who's who among the elite."

Jameson's tone of pride made it clear he thought that was a good thing. Kinley wasn't so certain. In her experience, the people who held all the power and money were rarely all good. They might not be all evil either, but…

Considering her brother and his two business partners were all ex-convicts—wealthy, influential and connected though they might be—she had her suspicions about what kind of clients they worked with.

"But you're not exclusive." It wasn't a question. She was fully aware Joker freelanced.

"No, but more and more I find myself occupied with their jobs. I'm in the position to be picky with what I take on."

He'd always been that way. In their field, Joker was a legend. He'd built a reputation for turning down highly lucrative jobs. He was mysterious and unpredictable. Which was part of the reason he'd been so successful over the years.

"I hope chasing after my money won't interfere with any other projects you have." Kinley smiled through the words, although she really didn't mean them.

Jameson's answering smile was pure humor. "No worries, *cucciola*. I can multitask."

Indignation bubbled through her chest. "I'm no puppy."

The twinkle in his pale green eyes irritated the hell out of her. The bastard was laughing at her.

"You should fire your Italian instructor."

"I taught myself Italian, thank you very much." Because she'd landed in a country without knowing the language and had needed to learn fast. She'd been pretty proud of her language skills. Until the deep roll of his chuckle scraped along her nerves.

"Then you need to brush up on your terms of endearment."

A hot flush suffused her body, followed by a cold rush. Nope, she was not going there right now. "When can I have access to a computer? I need to get to work tracking my money."

Slowly, Jameson shook his head.

Kinley's eyebrows pulled together in a deep frown. "What do you mean, no?" There was no way this man had stranded her in the Gulf of Mexico without access to a computer.

"I mean, there's no way I'm letting you touch my system. And if you're honest and the roles were reversed, you wouldn't let me near your equipment, either."

Kinley opened her mouth to argue but snapped her lips tightly together. Because damn him, he was right. He was too smart and her system wasn't just a patchwork of hardware cobbled together for access to the internet. Letting him get his sticky fingers on her equipment would give him the opportunity to dig into things she didn't want him to dig into.

"I brought my own computer." It wasn't nearly as powerful as his system, but it would do in a pinch. "Just give me internet access."

A single eyebrow rose in silent question. Yeah, she wouldn't do that either. With their skill set, network access would be just as deadly. Crap.

"I'm not just going to sit here and do nothing, Joker."

Jameson snagged a wineglass from the bar beside him. Reaching down, he ran the rough pads of his fingers over the center of her palm as he opened her fist. Placing the cool glass in her hand, he gently folded her fingers around it. Her hand, caught between the icy glass and the heat of his palm, wanted to tremble. But she refused to let it.

Bending over, Jameson looked straight into her eyes. A flutter of something rolled through her chest. Apprehension. Doubt. Certainly not interest. "It's just for a day or two. I'm sure you can find something to entertain yourself with."

Innuendo and heat flashed through his eyes. Was he really suggesting what she thought he was?

Part of her wanted to be pissed off at his audacity. But it was difficult to dredge up the emotion when her belly was melting and tingles of awareness crackled across her skin.

Never one to shy away from an issue, Kinley decided to confront him head-on. Raising an eyebrow of her own, she lounged against the railing, pursed her lips and cocked her head sideways. "Are you offering to be my boy toy?"

His laughter was genuine and bright. It lit up his face and made the butterflies in her belly beat their wings even faster. Her mouth tingled and the rest of her body hummed with a yearning she hadn't felt in a very long time.

Such a pain in the ass that this man would be the one her libido would decide to want.

"No. I don't trust you with my equipment, either my computers or my sensitive body parts."

"What? You think I'd go praying mantis on you?"

The corners of his eyes crinkled even as he held up his hands. "I hope not? But we don't like each other, so something tells me sex between us would be more of a fight than enjoyment."

She wanted to argue with him—her body knew exactly what kind of enjoyment they could share—but realized that wouldn't exactly help her. In fact, it would prove his point.

"Fine, you're not going to entertain me with that gorgeous body of yours." And she had no doubt it was stellar. "I'm just supposed to what, swim laps, read a book, play solitaire?"

"If you enjoy those things." Rachel appeared in the entry to the lounge. She didn't say anything, but Jameson acknowledged her with a flick of a single finger. With a nod, she melted away. "But for now, let's start with dinner. Rachel is a phenomenal chef."

She'd just bet the other woman was. Something told her Jameson didn't bother with anything that wasn't phenomenal.

* * *

Dinner was a production. Normally, he didn't bother with pomp and circumstance when he was aboard. The staff had learned quickly that when he was on the *Queen* what he wanted was peace and quiet. To relax and escape.

While he loved what he did, he often worked on high-pressure situations. Kidnappings, wrongful convictions, corporate espionage and national security. Some provided him money—excellent money—others gave him personal satisfaction. All were important, or he wouldn't take on the cases and clients. But they often left him carrying stress that he needed to relieve.

The formal dining area was adjacent to the main salon, decorated in shades of gray, white and pops of bloodred. What else would the *Queen of Hearts* be wearing?

Bright white light glowed from the hidden fixtures along the wall and beneath the built-in cabinetry and furniture. He rarely used the space. It was simply too formal for him. On the rare occasion Jameson bothered to come in here he'd often thought about redecorating to something more…him. But so far, he hadn't bothered. The ship was huge and there were plenty of spaces he did use.

And he'd told the staff a long time ago that they should use the formal salon for their own purposes and meals.

Which could explain why Rachel had simply given him a smirk when he'd informed her that he and Kinley would be eating there tonight. She hadn't said a word, but her expression spoke volumes.

Clearly, the staff assumed there was something between him and Kinley, which was fine. He didn't really care what they thought. But it would make things easier if no one questioned why they were on board.

It also explained why Rachel had outdone herself with a seven-course meal, something he'd never asked for in his life. But he had to admit, the woman could cook. She was a classically trained chef and damn good at her job.

She'd just set dishes in front of them, perfectly piped cream between layers of flaky pastry, berry compote and topped with a glistening honey-and-raspberry glaze. Artful swirls decorated the plate and his mouth watered for the first bite.

"You're looking at that dessert like a starving man. How is that possible? We've spent the past hour and a half eating delicious food."

Kinley had been quiet for most of the meal. At first, he'd tried to pull her out into conversation, but her one-word answers had quickly clued him in that she wasn't interested.

"Oh, now you want to talk and ask questions?"

Her grimace should have knocked some of the appeal off her gorgeous face. It didn't. It simply made her look cute…and more approachable. She'd come on board with whatever was stuffed inside the single suitcase she'd carried with her. And yet somehow, she sat beside him, the picture of poise and elegance.

It wasn't difficult to believe that Kinley belonged on the expensive yacht.

"No, really. You're about to devour that thing in one bite, aren't you?"

With a shrug, Jameson picked up his fork. "What can I say? I have a sweet tooth," he said, as he shoveled in a huge bite. His eyes closed in absolute adoration. The flaky pastry crumbled in his mouth, giving a balance to the texture of the silky cream. The tartness of the berries cut the sweetness and he could swear there was a hint of citrus somewhere.

Opening his eyes, the first thing he saw was Kinley, staring at him. Her own gorgeous blue eyes devoured him, a mixture of stunned and fascinated. Her own fork, laden with a more modest bite of dessert, hung suspended in the air, tragically forgotten and ignored.

There was a part of him that was proud at leaving her speechless. Leaning forward, he took the opportunity to snag the treat right off her fork.

"Hey," she exclaimed, yanking it out of his reach. "Too slow."

Shaking her head, she tucked her hand around her plate and inched farther down the table. "Mine."

Tension and annoyance had been drifting off Kinley since she'd sat. The longer the meal, the more it became clear that she wasn't thrilled to be sitting there with him.

His move, completely selfish and with no forethought, had cracked through the layers of those emotions. Her lips, delectable as they were, now curved with the tiniest hint of a smile.

Glaring over at him, she said, "I'm sure Rachel has more in the kitchen if your greed and gluttony are too much to ignore."

"Galley."

"What?"

"On board the ship it isn't a kitchen. It's a galley."

That hint of a grin grew as she rolled her eyes. "Whatever."

God, that grin was…rare and tempting. It took everything he had not to lean forward to kiss her and claim a piece of it for himself.

Nope, not the move he should make. There was no doubt in his mind the minute he tried she'd ram a fist into his face.

Oh, there were sparks between them. Undeniably. He'd been intrigued by her for months. But they lived in different worlds. She was a nomad and he'd spent a long time developing the roots that had been jerked out from under him when he was a kid.

Not to mention her estranged brother was one of his good friends.

Oh, and she didn't exactly like him.

So, those sparks…inconvenient. And unactionable.

Reaching behind him, Jameson snagged the bottle of wine tucked into a bucket of ice. Kinley had been nursing a single glass since they'd sat. Topping it off, he indicated she should drink.

The rest of the meal finished in silence, but it was

no longer filled with tension. The air between them was…almost comfortable.

Until Eric appeared in the doorway to the salon. Crossing the plush carpet, he paused at Jameson's shoulder and leaned over to whisper in his ear.

Frowning up at the other man, he responded. "Are you sure?"

With a nod, Eric stared at him with grave eyes. "Yes, sir."

Just as he'd expected, Kinley couldn't help herself but ask, "What's going on?"

"Nothing for you to worry about."

From the corner of his eye, he watched as pure anger rushed across Kinley's face.

"I am not some weak girl you can dismiss, Jameson Neally. If there's a problem I want to know about it. Has someone followed us?"

For a brief moment, he felt bad at the realization of her fear. "No, nothing like that."

Stepping back, Eric clasped his hands behind him and waited until Jameson nodded his approval. "The ship has experienced an engine malfunction."

Kinley's eyes narrowed. "What does that mean? Were we sabotaged?"

"No. Normal wear and tear a ship like this occasionally experiences, despite our best efforts at routine maintenance. Our engineer has diagnosed the problem and ordered a part, but it will take several days to arrive and be brought out to us."

"Several days?" Kinley stood up from her chair, half in and half out of it like she wanted to run. But there was nowhere to go.

Reaching over, Jameson laid a hand over hers. "We're fine. We were planning to be out to sea for a day or two anyway."

"That was your plan, but not mine. I need to find my money. The money you stole from me and lost. I can't do that stranded on a boat in the middle of the ocean when you won't let me near a computer or network."

"Ship and gulf."

"I'm sorry?"

"We're on a ship, not a boat, and we're in the Gulf of Mexico, not the ocean."

Her eyes widened and beneath his own hand hers trembled. Jameson realized it wasn't fear, but fury when fire and heat flashed across her expression.

"I want off this *ship*," she emphasized the word, "now."

"I'm sorry, ma'am, but that's not possible. We've dropped our anchor and won't be able to move until the part arrives and the engine is repaired."

"Can't someone come out to pick us up?"

Jameson looked over at Eric. "They could, but there's no reason to."

Her voice dipped low. "The reason is I want off."

Jameson squeezed her hand in the hopes it might dispel the worry that lurked beneath the screen of her anger. "Kinley, this changes nothing."

Her eyes narrowed even more as she yanked her hand away. "Let me understand, you're trapping me here?"

If he was honest, he'd trapped her on the *Queen*

the moment she stepped on board, but he wasn't about
to admit that to her.

"Hardly…we're just delayed."

Standing, she pressed her fists to the gleaming
surface of the table and leaned in, inches from his
face. Her anger burned. The evidence of it clear in
her gleaming eyes.

Which made her quiet statement all the more con-
cerning. "A gilded cage is still a cage, Jameson. You
more than most should understand that."

Four

There was something fishy about the exchange between Joker and the captain.

How does a twenty-five-million-dollar yacht break? Didn't they have regular maintenance or something? The whole situation felt highly convenient.

Her mind had been working the problem since she'd walked away from dinner. Staring up at the ceiling of her stateroom, she'd expected that the unhappy circumstances and unfamiliar setting would keep her awake half the night. But apparently the gentle rocking of the ship had lulled her to sleep.

But her eyes had popped open this morning and her brain had started spinning again.

Her gut was telling her things weren't right, but she had no proof. Nothing to substantiate the sensation, except instinct. The same instincts that had kept her safe for the past twelve years.

Really, longer than that. Kinley had grown up surrounded by liars and criminals. Self-preservation had developed a sixth sense for when someone was lying to her…and Jameson had been ringing all the warning bells.

What really pissed her off was how Jameson kept trying to control her life. He'd manipulated her by stealing her money, under the guise of protecting her. She didn't need protection—she'd been taking care of herself for a long time—but definitely not his brand of protection.

If she'd wanted to be under someone's thumb, always manipulated, ignored and lied to, she would have stayed with her parents.

The more she learned about Jameson, the more she saw him as a replica of them. Clearly, he was manipulative. He lived this clandestine, mysterious life, hiding who he truly was. Everything was a facade. Take the yacht for instance… The man had money, but until Kinley stepped foot on the ship, she wouldn't have guessed it from the way he lived.

Good guys didn't have to hide who they were.

Unfortunately, her body reacted in inconvenient ways whenever Jameson was close. Which irritated the hell out of her. For God's sake, she should be able to control her reaction.

But maybe she could use it to her advantage.

Yes, there was chemistry between them. They were stuck on this yacht—which in and of itself pissed her off—and made it very difficult to avoid him. So she'd use the only advantage she had.

Kinley stared at the wardrobe, fully stocked with clothing that no doubt would perfectly fit her. How he'd managed to get all this on board amazed her. And, if forced to admit it, scared her a little.

For some perverse reason, her gaze was drawn to a tiny, bright blue bikini. Maybe it was the color; it reminded her of the Aegean Sea and a little island in the Cyclades. The thing was barely more than strings and triangles of cloth held together with bubble gum and dreams. Never in her life would she think to wear something like this in public. But they weren't in public, were they? The gentle sway of the ship beneath her feet reminded her that she wasn't surrounded by people who might gawk.

Sure, the staff was there, but she already knew they were too polite to comment or care what she wore. Or didn't wear.

Contemplating last night, their dinner and the tense chemistry between them, Kinley thought, *what the hell*, and snatched the bikini from the hanger.

She almost changed her mind when she looked at her reflection in the mirror. So much of her olive skin was on display that she had to fight the urge to cover herself with her hands. Nope, she wasn't going to do that.

Steeling her spine, Kinley hid the flash drive pendant she religiously wore, grabbed a towel from the stack in the closet and wound her way up the narrow staircase to the sundeck. The highest level of the ship, she could see the open water spread out in front of her. A pleasant breeze stirred the air and kept the sun from overheating the deck.

Dropping her towel on a lounge chair, Kinley didn't even bother testing the water before jumping into the plunge pool. Cool waves lapped against her exposed skin, sending goose bumps erupting across her body.

The length wasn't long enough to really swim or exercise, but it was deep enough to cover her head and cool off. Holding her breath, she stayed under until her lungs felt tight with the need for air. Bursting through the surface, she took in a huge gulp of oxygen, her eyes closed to the bright light. Sweeping her hair back, she tilted her face up.

Peace settled over her, dissolving the tension that was her constant companion.

"What do you think you're doing?"

Until his voice disrupted the quiet.

Squinting, Kinley put a shielding hand over her eyes. "I should think that would be obvious."

Irritation and an unholy awareness rolled through Jameson's belly. He'd nearly swallowed his tongue when Kinley had walked out onto that deck in that swimsuit.

It wasn't that he hadn't been aware of her body, because he absolutely had been. She was tall and slender. Curvy in all the right places. But recognizing that because he could infer the details beneath her clothes was completely different from seeing almost every inch of her skin on display.

"You're naked, Kinley." The words blasted out of his mouth like little bullets of accusation, way more forceful than he'd meant them to be.

But apparently, they bounced right off their intended target. Shrugging, Kinley rose from the pool and plopped into one of the loungers. She picked up the sunglasses she'd dropped onto the table before sliding the large lenses over her eyes. "I'm not. I'm wearing one of the swimsuits your people left me."

He would have to talk to Meg about what constituted appropriate attire.

"It doesn't even cover your ass." He should know. He'd stared at the round, firm globes of her rear as she'd walked across the deck. The material bisected the curve of her butt before disappearing into the crack.

"If it bothers you, don't look."

Ha! Like that was an option. He knew he shouldn't want her, but logic didn't seem to work around Kinley. She was here against her will. She didn't like him. And even if maybe she felt the same draw that he did, in the long run it wouldn't matter. The first chance she had, Kinley would be gone.

Because she didn't stay.

But her flippant attitude wasn't helping. Neither was the semihard ridge of his erection fighting against the fly of his jeans. They'd been damn roomy a few minutes ago. Shifting his hips, Jameson tried to find some relief, but there was none.

The front view of her suit might have been even worse than the back. Strings connected the tiny triangles of material, barely big enough to disguise the color of her nipples, before coming together to tie at her neck.

Reaching behind her, Kinley snagged at the end of the knot. The strings slithered along her body and the triangles flipped down to join them.

Jameson stood, feet welded to the deck, for several seconds. Before the thought had even formed in his head, his body leaped forward. Grabbing a towel from the stack close by, he snapped it open, stooped and covered her with it.

It was either that or snatch her up and kiss the hell out of her, something he really didn't need to do.

Legs folded, he crouched beside her lounger. His upper body draped across her as their faces met, nose to nose.

"What are you doing?"

"Absolutely nothing." They were so close that the warmth of her breath brushed across his cheek. A buzzing started in the back of his brain and swept beneath the surface of his skin.

The warmth of the sun beat against his back. Heat spread through him.

"That's bullshit and we both know it."

Kinley shrugged. "What are you going to do about it?"

Her mouth was so close. His gaze zeroed in on her lips. The shape of them. The tempting way her upper lip bowed in the center. The tip of her tongue swept out, deliberately wetting her bottom lip before disappearing.

He wanted to dive after it. Coax her out with his own tongue. Taste every inch of her gleaming skin.

Jameson waited for her to push him away. To yell at him. Something.

Time slowed to the space in between his racing heartbeats. His brain blared at him, so many reasons why he shouldn't go there. Why he shouldn't start this. Because once he had a taste of her, he was worried he might not be able to stop.

She was the one playing with fire, but something deep inside told him he was the one destined to get burned. "To hell with it," he growled, more to himself than to her, before taking what he'd wanted.

The moment his mouth touched hers he was lost. All coherent thought fled. The buzz in his blood ramped higher, drowning out every sound and sensation except her.

For several seconds she simply lay there, accepting what he was giving her. But that didn't last long. Leaning up, Kinley opened her mouth and let him in. No, she did more than that. She made demands all her own.

The thrill of her, the taste of her, the way she met each stroke of his tongue with an answering one of her own. Her fists found his hair and buried deep, tugged. She used her hold to command him in a way that sent a thrill straight through to his toes.

The towel, forgotten by them both, slithered into her lap. His hands brushed up her arms and down her chest until he could fill his palm with her breast. Her skin was warm, not just from the sun, but from the same heat burning through him.

His fingers found the tight bud of her nipple and tugged. A mewling sound vibrated through her throat. Jameson drank it in and wanted more. Beneath his fingers, Kinley arched, silently asking for the same thing. And he had no problem giving it to them both.

Drowning—he was drowning in her. The sensation was tempting, disconcerting and disorienting at the same time.

Her hands roamed across his chest. Reaching for the hem of his shirt, damp from touching her wet body, she searched for his naked skin. Jameson closed his eyes, pure bliss, as the pads of her fingers brushed across his chest. Her fingers played over his ribs and abs, not light, but not hesitant. Exploring, taking, demanding.

There was nothing tentative about Kinley. She wanted the heat building between them, and her actions made that clear.

A sound from across the deck broke through the haze of desire blocking out everything else.

Twisting, Jameson realized one of the staff must have slipped onto the deck, leaving the platter of meat, cheese, crackers and fruit that he'd instructed be sent up to Kinley before he'd seen her and followed her onto the deck.

The interruption served as a cold dose of reality. What was he thinking?

It had been a hell of a long time since he'd let anything overwhelm him into making rash—and bad—decisions. Hell, he was still paying for some of those mistakes. He really didn't need to add any more to the list. Especially with his friend's little sister.

Turning to her, Jameson eased away. "I'm sorry." Although he wasn't certain if he was apologizing to her or himself.

God, she made it hard to do the right thing. He had a new tattoo of his zipper along the throbbing length of his erection as proof.

Sprawling in her chair, Kinley crossed her arms behind her head, thrusting her breasts at him like a smorgasbord, and gave him a lopsided, devilish grin. "No apology needed."

She didn't bother to grab the towel or the ties to her top. She sat there, half-naked and practically daring him to do something about it.

But he couldn't. Wouldn't.

She resented him—not that he could blame her— which meant that this little endeavor was a stunt to try to manipulate him. He understood the effort, even if it left him with an inconvenient problem tenting his jeans.

Kinley felt out of control right now, because she was. She was used to living in a world of chaos where she solved problems, chased bad guys and righted wrongs that weren't hers to shoulder. And he'd taken all that away from her, at least for a few days.

So he couldn't take advantage of the situation.

Not to mention her brother would kill him if he discovered that Joker had found her, stolen her money, practically kidnapped her and then screwed her brains out.

Because if he got his hands on her again that's exactly what would happen.

Jameson pulled in a deep breath, searched for a center of resolve, and finding it, said, "Please cover up." His words were guttural and deep, but he'd managed to voice them so that was a win.

"No."

"Excuse me?"

Kinley cocked her head. Soft strands of her dark hair escaped from the knot she'd tied it into and tickled across her cheek. Jameson wanted to wrap his fist in the tangled tresses and pull her against his body.

"No, I won't cover up. I won't make this easier for you. I don't care if I make you uncomfortable. You've manipulated me, stranded me, stolen from me and lied to me."

He couldn't argue with her, although she was taking everything he'd done and twisting it into the worst possible interpretation.

"You enjoyed that kiss, professor. We both did. If I've learned one thing in my life, it's not to apologize for the things that I want and enjoy."

Had she really? From where he was standing, outside her life and looking in for months, he'd say there was very little in her life that she allowed herself to enjoy.

But now wasn't the time to call her on the lie.

Instead, he went with another truth. "Your brother wouldn't appreciate me fucking you."

Her mouth went flat and so did her eyes. "I don't care what Gray would or wouldn't appreciate. He isn't a part of my life."

"By your choice, Kinley. He wants to be, but he

won't push you. He understands what you've been through."

A soft scoffing sound scraped through her throat. "Sure he does."

How the hell had they gotten here? One minute they were devouring each other, the next they were discussing her brother. At least the discussion had lessened the ache in his cock.

Either way, sticking around right now wasn't going to do either of them any good. With a sigh, Jameson rose. Without another word, he walked away. The best thing he could do right now was find Kinley's money. The sooner he did that, the sooner she'd return to the nomadic, complicated, tumultuous life that she led and the temptation to keep her would be gone.

Then he'd let Gray know where he could find her and the two could work their issues out themselves. Without him stuck in the middle.

Kinley watched him go, a combination of disappointment, frustration and heat mixing through her blood. The man was dangerous. In more ways than one.

She didn't want to want him, but apparently her body had different ideas. The buzz in her blood told her being with him was inevitable. Oh, if she could avoid him, then maybe she could avoid the outcome. But stuck on the yacht with him…she didn't have the willpower.

Or the desire.

They were both grown adults, unattached and interested. Sure, they were messy in so many ways. But that didn't stop the need throbbing low in her body.

And if sleeping with him was inevitable, then at least Kinley wanted to control the circumstances around it. She wanted to benefit in more ways than the amazing orgasm that was no doubt in her future.

Clearly, she'd pushed his buttons. So maybe tonight she'd push a couple more. Satisfied with her plan, Kinley settled into her lounger.

She might have millions of dollars in her bank account—no, *had*—but she never really allowed herself to enjoy the lifestyle that came with it. She didn't stay at high-priced hotels or luxury resorts. The only reason she owned fast cars was because one day she might need speed to get away. And, okay, she enjoyed the effervescent hit of adrenaline they provided.

But she didn't own a mansion. Hell, she didn't even own a three-bedroom rancher. She rented wherever she went and paid in cash whenever possible. She splurged on IT equipment, buying the best of the best, but other than that, Kinley lived a simple life.

Today, she took advantage of the luxury at her fingertips. She enjoyed being waited on. She dozed in the sun, floated in the pool and relaxed in the hot tub.

To add the right spin to her ruse, she made sure to request a steady stream of fruity drinks all day… and then proceeded to surreptitiously dispose of them while no one was looking. If the staff was reporting to Jameson—and she had no doubt they were—hopefully they would indicate that she should be three sheets to the wind.

It had taken everything she had to pretend to be relaxed and uncaring. In reality, she'd been bored out of her mind. Thinking back, Kinley couldn't remember a single day in the past twelve years that she'd been completely idle. Her fingers itched for a keyboard and her brain spun with thoughts and ideas she couldn't do anything about.

When the sun started to sink into the horizon, Kinley let out a quiet sigh of relief. Gathering her things, she headed to her stateroom. After a shower, she took time to primp, something else she rarely bothered with. Hair and makeup done, she stared at her reflection in the mirror.

Tilting her head sideways, she objectively cataloged herself. All her life she'd been compared to her mother, a vibrant showgirl with the punch of stunning beauty. She wasn't like Cece, her mother, and had been reminded of that constantly as a young girl. Oh, she was pretty enough, but not showstopping. Not headliner material.

Not that Kinley cared. While her mother had bemoaned her daughter's lack of beauty and sophistication, Kinley had never wanted that life. She was perfectly content with who she was.

Her dark hair and olive skin worked together. Her almond shaped eyes gave her an air of mystery that tonight she'd played up with perfectly applied liner and powders. Her lips were painted a deep, sultry red that made the blue of her eyes pop.

Kinley had taken the time to curl her long, straight hair into subtle waves that added movement and volume around her face. The ends brushed just past her breasts, following the natural curves of her body.

Reaching into the closet, she pulled out a deceptively simple black dress. On the hanger, it looked common enough. Who didn't own a little black dress, right? But once she slipped it on…it was clear the designer knew what she was about.

The hem hit just below her knees but a wide vee slit up to barely below her hip on one side. The material hugged her body perfectly, outlining her curves in all the right places. The neckline was sweetheart, the pendant flash drive settling into the hollow it created. The fabric widened to sweep up and over one shoulder.

Classic, but dramatic, exactly what she loved. Not for the first time, Kinley thought that Jameson's staff were damn good at their job. And a little scary. How had they known exactly what she might need before leaving the dock?

Shaking her head, Kinley sat on the bed, tucked her feet to the side and fastened the tiny strap around her ankle for the Louboutin Aribak stilettos. The leather T-strap and bow at the ankle were the perfect little touch of something to pair with the dress.

Rubbing her lips together, Kinley headed out of her stateroom and upstairs for the salon. Just like last night, gold light sparkled off gleaming surfaces, strategically placed mirrors, and expensive crystal, china and fixtures.

Before she could say anything, one of Rachel's staff appeared by her side with a flute of champagne and indicated a selection of appetizers set on a built-in beneath the wall of windows. "Mr. Neally will be here shortly. He asked you to make yourself comfortable."

Accepting the glass, Kinley allowed herself a large swallow. The sparkling wine effervesced in her mouth, rolling down her throat in a fruity, pleasant rush. She'd decided to give herself two glasses with dinner. Not enough to impair her judgment, but enough that Jameson would think she was still well on her way to being inebriated.

Besides, the wine might help settle her nerves. It wasn't that she was uneasy, more on edge. That unsettling sensation right before you go into an interview for your dream job. Excited but apprehensive and slightly unsure.

Kinley was standing at the wall of windows, staring out at the water and the endless dark sky above it, when he walked into the room. She didn't even need his reflection in the window to know he'd arrived.

Her body told her.

The energy running beneath the surface of her skin amped up, almost as if someone had touched her with a live wire. Gritting her teeth, Kinley forced herself not to turn around. She waited for him to come to her; after all, tonight would be a bit of cat and mouse...the same game they'd been playing virtually for months.

Slipping up beside her, Jameson was careful to leave plenty of space between them. But she'd watched his wavy expression in the glass as he'd approached. The way his gaze had sharpened as it swept along her body sent a thrill racing down her spine.

Twisting her head, Kinley held her glass of champagne in one hand as she studied him. The man was gorgeous in an unexpected way. Tonight, he'd gathered his rich, caramel-colored hair into a knot at the back of his head. He'd trimmed his beard so it skimmed the sides of his cheeks. His strong mouth stayed in a straight line, neither a frown nor a smile.

But his eyes, God, they made her burn. Heat and hunger glittered through the pale green depths as he simply watched her. He didn't use words to tell her that she was beautiful, but then he didn't need to. The way he looked at her said enough.

Did they even need to eat dinner? In that moment, the only thing she was hungry for was him.

Kinley opened her mouth to say something, although she wasn't entirely certain what, but Rachel's entrance into the salon backed the words up in her throat.

"Dinner is served," she said as two staff members entered behind her carrying domed plates and dishes. They arranged everything on the dining table at the far end of the room before disappearing again.

"After you," Jameson said, accompanied by a sweeping gesture for her to move ahead of him.

Grasping her chair, he pulled it out before moving to his own. He sat at the head of the table while she occupied the chair to his right.

"How's the search for my money?"

Joker didn't even look up as he responded. "Still missing, but I'm following a few leads. Clearly, whoever it is knows what they're doing because they covered their tracks."

"I hope so."

"What's that supposed to mean?"

"It would be embarrassing if an amateur bested you, wouldn't it?"

Jameson's lips twisted into a grimace, but he didn't contradict her. "Can you provide me a list of people who might have a vendetta against you?"

Kinley laughed, the sound short and humorless. "That would be a long list."

"I already know several," he mused, "but thought I'd see if I'd missed any over the years."

There was a part of her irritated that he'd been digging into her life, exhuming her past and studying it like she was some subject to be dissected. The rest of her was intrigued to find out just how far—and deep into her past—he'd gone.

Had he discovered all her secrets?

Chewing thoughtfully on a bite of perfectly prepared steak, she made a considering sound. "You know, it would be faster if you just gave me access and let me help you."

This time Jameson's lip twitch turned into a rueful smile. "Not on your life."

Kinley shrugged, grabbed the bottle of wine sitting in a bucket in the center of the table and poured herself another glass. "Had to try. I'll put together a list later and have it for you in the morning."

"Excellent."

She sent him a smile and a salute with her full glass. "I have a vested interest in your success."

"No." Leaning forward, Jameson plucked the glass from her fingers and placed it on the table out of her reach. "What you have is a driving need to court danger and atone for sins that aren't yours because you won't confront the real source of your guilt."

Five

Jameson watched as Kinley's perfect complexion flushed red with anger. But he had to hand it to her, she kept a lid on the building pressure of it.

Her lips thinned and her gorgeous blue eyes flashed. "Thank you for your expert analysis of my life and motives, even though it wasn't requested." Reaching around him, she snagged the glass he'd taken from her and purposely took a large swallow.

It didn't escape his notice that she didn't argue with his point though.

And his tactic had worked because she was no longer trying to figure out a way into his server room.

Yes, Kinley had a vested interest in what he was doing, but that was obvious enough and he hadn't needed her to point that fact out. Which wasn't why she'd said it.

Kinley was cunning. She had amazing instincts and had taught herself the skills she used to topple criminal empires. She was impressive and he knew with a few phone calls she could have job offers from multiple agencies and private companies.

She *chose* the life she led. Danger, upheaval, constantly looking over her shoulder and moving from place to place. She'd been operating in survival mode for so long that he was pretty certain she didn't recognize or acknowledge friendship. She most certainly didn't trust.

But then he couldn't really blame her.

Gray hadn't spoken to him about what he'd gone through. He hadn't needed to since Joker had been the one to find the crumbs leading to his birth mother, the criminal she'd hooked her claws into and the surprise half sister he'd never known. Until that night, he hadn't been aware of his father's affair or that the woman he'd grown up calling mom wasn't his biological mother.

Cece, Gray and Kinley's mother, had abandoned him for a payout…because she spent her entire life taking everything she could get.

Jameson didn't need to live the experience to understand that the people who raised Kinley were trash. The fact that she'd run away the first chance she had said more than enough.

There was a part of him that hated what she'd gone through. No kid should have to deal with that kind of life. But it happened. He'd seen plenty of bad situations in his years in foster care after his parents' deaths. Hell, he'd been in those situations a time or two.

But both he and Kinley had turned out okay. Depending on your definition of okay.

Kinley tipped her head, long throat swallowing a huge gulp of the wine she'd just poured. According to his staff, she'd been drinking pretty much non-stop all day. Which was uncharacteristic, although he supposed he hadn't given her much else to occupy herself with.

Although after spending the last hour with her, he hadn't seen a single sign that she was truly impaired. No slurred speech, no unsteady movements. A part of him wondered if she'd been dumping his liquor over the side of the ship when no one was looking.

Pushing her plate away, Kinley leaned into her chair and watched him over the rim of her glass. A half smile curled the edges of her lips, making him both wary and aroused at the same time.

"So, you won't give me details."

He'd never said that, but contradicting her wouldn't gain him anything, so he kept his mouth shut.

Standing up, she pushed her chair away from the table. Soft strains of mood music drifted through the room, background noise that seemed to accompany her as she moved.

Pushing his plate away, Kinley propped her hips against the edge of the table.

"Maybe I wasn't done with that," he mused.

She flashed him an unapologetic grin and crowded into his personal space. He had absolutely zero desire to move, though he probably should have. Tipping his head, Jameson watched her. And waited.

What game was she playing?

Wrapping her foot around the leg of his chair, she used her higher height to pull him closer. His knees bumped against hers before spreading wide. She placed both feet on either side of his hips, caging him in. The skirt she'd worn into dinner slithered against her skin, revealing the long expanse of creamy thigh.

His palms glided up the sloping curve of her calves to settle on the inside of her thighs. The warmth of her skin burned into the center of each hand. His fingers tightened, although he wasn't sure if he was preparing to hold her still or push her away.

"My shoes are pinching. Would you mind unbuckling them for me?"

The question was innocent enough, but the fire in her eyes hardly matched.

Jameson didn't move. His body was strung tight, caught between what he wanted—the woman clearly on display—and what he should do—push her away.

"What are you playing at?"

Slowly, the tip of Kinley's pink tongue brushed across the curve of her bottom lip, leaving a glistening trail he wanted to follow with his own.

"I'm not playing." Her words were strong, but beneath them was a breathy quality that told him she might want to be steady, but was far from it.

Which should have settled his own pounding heart, but only made it race faster.

"Kinley, you need to stand up and walk away. Now."

For both their sakes. His control was hanging by a very precarious thread. All the warnings he'd given himself earlier, the reasons he'd stacked up not to touch her, were disappearing like smoke.

Oh, they were still true, but Jameson was no longer certain he had the strength to care. There was no way this would end well—for either of them—but if she was hell-bent on giving him no choice…

Leaning forward, she dropped her voice to a whisper. "What will happen if I don't?"

Well, he'd warned her.

Surging up from his chair, Jameson wrapped one hand around her nape and the other arm around her waist. It was nothing to sweep her off her perch on the table and into his arms. It was easy to use his fist wrapped in her hair to tilt her head so that he could claim her mouth.

The sound she made when his lips touched hers… pure unadulterated need. And the punch of her taste lit up his senses like nothing he'd ever experienced before.

Kinley Sullivan was hardly meek or docile. Oh, no, she was fire in his arms.

Her legs tightened around his waist and her own hands made demands, tearing at his clothes. Her tongue warred with his, fighting for an upper hand both of them wanted and neither would get.

Suddenly, her hands pushed against his chest, forcing air between them. "Wait. Wait."

Jameson immediately stopped, stilling his hands from blindly exploring every inch of her body that he could reach.

Kinley's labored breaths worked in and out of her lungs. He could feel the fast flutter of her pulse beneath his thumb as it rested along the side of her throat. Her gaze raced across his face, although he wasn't sure what she was looking for. Reassurance? She'd never struck him as the kind of woman who needed it, but then maybe he didn't really know her.

And maybe he really wanted to.

He would have backed away and given her space, but her legs were still wrapped tight around his hips and no matter what, he wouldn't drop her.

He should have kept his hands in place, but he couldn't stop himself from stroking that thumb along the side of her throat. Her skin was soft. So silky. And the electric jolt of touching her was addictive.

"What? What do you need, Kinley? What do you want?"

Her eyes closed for the briefest moment before popping open again. "I don't know." Something told him that up until this point, she'd been playing a game. But this, those words, were real. They seemed to be pulled from deep inside her soul, a secret she didn't want to share, but couldn't seem to stop.

"That's okay. You don't have to. Unwrap your legs and I'll put you down. Walk away."

Instead of listening to him, she shook her head. "I can't."

"Can't or won't?"

"Does it matter? Isn't it the same thing?"

"No, it's the difference between physically being able to and mentally being able to."

Her burst of laughter tickled across his skin. "Fine, then won't."

And that was all he needed to know. "If that changes, just let me know."

Cradling her against his chest, Jameson walked through the salon and into the hallway and headed straight for his stateroom.

She wouldn't let him go and even if he should, he really didn't want her to.

This was supposed to have been a little bit of foreplay. Distraction. A power play to gain the upper hand. But everything backfired on her the minute Jameson touched her.

The low, slow burn of desire that she'd been telling herself wasn't real had blazed into a full-fledged inferno that she couldn't ignore or escape. And, she had to admit, he'd given her plenty of opportunity to walk away. But she didn't want to. No, she wanted him. Now. Despite everything between them.

Or maybe because of it.

Kinley rarely let herself indulge in sex. It was messy. She'd never been built for one-night stands, but she couldn't afford anything else. Jameson was different. There were no pretenses, just need and desire.

She wanted him and it was gratifying to know he wanted her, too.

The moment the stateroom door shut behind them, Kinley's feet hit the floor. Jameson wasted no time in backing her through the room until her knees hit the edge of the king-size bed. His mouth found hers again and everything around her dulled. Everything except him.

The heat of him. The enticing scent—musk, male and something faintly metallic. His teeth found her bottom lip and gently tugged even as his hands released the zipper at the back of her dress.

The material fell from her shoulders and brushed against her legs as it fluttered to the ground, a tempting caress all its own.

And that's when he took a step back.

Kinley stood in nothing but her lacy bra and matching panties. Her hair tumbled over her shoulder, tickling into the cups of her bra. Her breasts rose and fell against the tight material, threatening to spill over the edge with each ragged breath.

"God, you are absolutely stunning."

He wasn't the first man to tell her that, although he was the first one she actually believed. The way his heated gaze devoured her was hard to fabricate.

Reaching behind her, she found the clasp of her bra and unhooked it. "Thank you," she murmured as the straps slithered down her arms. She watched him visibly swallow when the bra fell away. Her nipples tightened and throbbed, begging for his attention.

"Touch me," she demanded. And Jameson didn't hesitate to comply.

"God, yes." He reached for her, filling his palms

with the round globes of her breasts. The rough rasp of his skin against hers sent tingles racing along her spine. When his thumb and finger found her puckered flesh and tugged…she nearly gasped at the zing of electricity centered right between her thighs.

Kinley wanted to see him, too, so while he continued to tug and tease, she managed to work the fly of his slacks and spread them wide. The ridge of his erection burned against her palm, insistent and intent.

Jameson hissed and then groaned, the sounds echoing through her own ears. Picking her up, he placed her in the center of the bed. Kinley pressed up onto her elbows as he stood, staring down at her. His expression was intense, his mouth pulled into a tight line.

"You're supposed to be enjoying this," she joked.

Shaking his head, he said, "Trust me, I'm enjoying this immensely." Cupping her heel, he deliberately unbuckled each shoe and let them fall to the floor with a clank.

Kneeling between her open thighs, he slowly let his fingers drift up her legs, calves, knees, thighs, until he grazed the crease of her hip. His finger dipped beneath the edge of her panties, playing against the skin that hid there.

Kinley's hips rolled up and off the bed, silently asking him for more. Hooking a finger into the edge of her panties, he pulled them slowly from her body.

The breeze brushed her naked sex, but the touch only served to tease her more. She wanted him. And because she did, she didn't hesitate to hold a hand out to him. To call him back.

She watched as he shed the rest of his clothes, the most amazing striptease she'd ever seen in her life. She'd known he was built beneath the T-shirts and jeans, but seeing it in person… Lord, have mercy.

"How can a man who spends hours in front of a computer have abs like that?"

He shrugged. "I do yoga."

"Bullshit."

A smile played at his lips. "It calms the mind and focuses the body."

"Whatever. If you want to lie to me now…"

The mattress depressed when his knee landed on the bed between her open thighs. He stalked up her body, stopping along the way to press hot, open-mouthed kisses against her skin. He sucked and nipped, and all the while her body burned. The rough drag of his beard against her sent sparks rippling beneath her skin. Kinley writhed against the sheets, lost in the sensations he was building inside her.

He finally reached her throat, pausing long enough to suck at the racing pulse buried there before whispering, "Nothing about this is going to be a lie, Kinley."

Everything inside her stilled. Because she believed him. And she couldn't remember a single time in her life when she'd wholly, completely believed another person. What sucked was that he might not think this was a lie, but she knew it was. Or it had started on a lie, even if it wasn't anymore.

Her head spun, because she was quickly losing the slippery grip on everything around her. What was right? What was wrong? She didn't know anymore. In any other situation, that loss of control would have had panic breathing down her neck. Right now, here, with Jameson…that didn't happen. In fact, a huge part of her wanted to just let go.

His fingers found the slick opening to her sex and pushed deep inside. And then nothing else mattered except the way he made her feel.

Kinley's hips vaulted off the bed even as a groan of pleasure escaped her tight throat. "God. More," she breathed, hoping he could actually hear the demand. Jameson teased her, thrusting in and out until her body was strung so tight she thought it would snap.

Finding her mouth with his, Jameson's tongue tangled with hers. "You're even more gorgeous when you let go," he breathed against her skin.

The orgasm hit her like a semi hurtling through a hurricane. Her entire body shook with the force of the release. But she didn't have any time to settle and savor because Jameson took the opportunity to thrust deep inside her.

The feel of him, on top of her already-sensitive system, launched her into another wave of release. "Holy hell," she breathed out as her body clung to his.

Jameson's hips rolled against hers with the steady rhythm of his thrusts. The fog filling her brain cleared enough for her to watch his expression of ecstasy as his own orgasm hit.

Something about the intimate, vulnerable moment

settled deep inside Kinley's chest. She wanted to wrap her arms around his shoulders and bury her face in the crook of his neck. And because the urge was so strong, she purposely rolled away.

Padding into the attached bathroom, she started the shower. Not because she needed one, but because she needed some space. Space to quash the tiny seed of *what-if* making the center of her chest ache.

But it wasn't to be.

Jameson followed her, disposing of the condom she'd been too far gone to even notice he'd grabbed. At least one of them had been thinking.

Stepping into the enclosed space, she let the hot water and steam rush across her body. Kinley was startled when the door to the enclosure opened and Jameson stepped in. The shower wasn't small, but it wasn't huge either. Two people fit, although it was a tight squeeze and there was no way to keep their bodies from brushing against each other.

Not that it mattered when he wrapped an arm around her waist from behind.

"You think too much," he said, right before his mouth found hers again.

Jameson watched Kinley as she pretended to sleep. Oh, he knew it was a ruse, but he wasn't about to call her on it. He wanted to see just how far she was willing to take this little game.

He had to admit, he hadn't expected her to go this far. And if he was a better man, he might have stopped things before they'd gotten here. But he wasn't a better man. In fact, he was downright terrible.

Because there was no denying he'd wanted her from the moment she walked into the basement of his house. And faced with what his body had been begging him to claim, he couldn't find the strength to say no or push her away.

In truth, this could blow up in his face. Kinley didn't trust him. She didn't trust anyone. She'd already called him on manipulating her, and if she found out he was still doing it, she'd be pissed.

But it was more than that.

He admired her. She was strong. Independent. Gifted and brilliant. And something deep inside his chest was tempted by the idea of her next to him.

She reminded him of his mother, which sent another tiny shard of grief and memory through his chest. Memories of her were of a happy, normal childhood. The life tragedy and circumstance stole from him.

He'd spent years trying to get back to that ideal in his head. The house in a neighborhood with a corner store and kids riding bikes down the sidewalk. And for years, he'd allowed himself to pretend.

On the surface, he'd bought himself exactly that. And then built a secret life he kept locked in the basement.

Kinley, she kept shattering his illusion.

Because despite everything, he could see her sitting on the front porch, waving at the neighbors with him.

But that wasn't who she was. Or who she wanted to be.

So this entire situation had just vaulted from messy

into downright chaotic. But no matter what, Jameson couldn't dredge up the guilt or regret for what had just happened. He'd pay later, but the price would be totally worth it.

For now, he would simply appreciate the moment for what it was. Because it wasn't likely to happen again.

Once Kinley was out of his bed and had what she wanted, she'd put those walls up between them again. The same walls she used to keep everyone out.

Kinley's breathing evened, even if he could tell by the thump of her pulse against his shoulder that she wasn't really asleep. To play along, Jameson shifted until he was more comfortable. His palm cupped the curve of her hip and he forced his own breathing to shallow. His muscles relaxed.

It wasn't long, maybe twenty minutes, before Kinley quietly slipped from his bed. Through slit eyes, he watched her gather her belongings without bothering to put any of her clothing back on.

The door cracked open, spilling white light across her gorgeous skin. In any other circumstances, he might have appreciated just how radiant she was.

But not many men would be joyful to watch a woman they'd just spent hours in bed with, sneaking away like a thief in the night.

Six

Holy hell. She hadn't expected *that*. Kinley's world was still spinning. Never in her life had anyone made her feel the way Jameson did. And it wasn't just the physical pleasure and unbelievable release. Releases, but who was counting?

It was more than that. The man knew how to make a woman feel…desired, powerful, sexy. Jameson Neally was a brilliant man and having all that intelligence and focus centered on her…

She'd never let anyone close enough to give her that. It was hard to connect to someone who didn't even know her real name. She'd never in her life expected to want it.

But, God, she did. She wanted him. More. Now.

Which was dangerous, stupid and inconvenient.

Kinley couldn't afford any of those things. She had to remember that her security was in the wind along with her money. She needed those millions. The money was her only safety net. And while a part of her was beginning to think spending the rest of her life on this yacht with Jameson might not be the worst thing in the world...the rest of her couldn't sacrifice her independence.

Not when she'd fought so hard and given up so much to find it. No man—or amount of unbelievably amazing sex—was worth that.

So things might have gotten a little carried away, but that didn't change the overall plan. In fact, it might make things easier. Jameson had let his guard down and she could use that to her advantage.

Rolling onto her belly, Kinley snuggled into the crook of his arm and rested her head on his shoulder. She let her eyelids fall closed as she drew mindless patterns across his chest. The tempting weight of his arm curled around her waist as his hand cupped the curve of her hip.

His warmth seeped beneath her skin, but she forced herself not to give in. Not to fall asleep in his arms.

Slowly, the rhythmic rise and fall of his chest beneath her cheek mellowed as Jameson fell asleep. The weight of his hand slipped, falling to the bed beside her with a thump.

Still, she waited another several minutes. Patience was a virtue, after all.

Her brain spun, guilt, irritation and a clawing need

for him mixing into a sludge deep in her belly. No, she would not feel bad about what she was about to do. This man had stolen from her. He'd tracked her and manipulated her.

She would not feel guilty for doing the same thing.

When she was certain he was asleep, Kinley quietly climbed from the bed. Jameson mumbled and shifted, his body settling into a more comfortable position now that she wasn't stretched beside him. But he didn't wake.

Kinley tiptoed through the dark room. Thank goodness every piece of furniture was bolted down so there was little to stub a toe on or stumble over. As she went, she grabbed up her dress, panties and shoes, scooping the entire mess into her arms.

She didn't let out the breath she was holding until the cabin door closed quietly behind her. She didn't bother to dress, but used the pile of clothes as a shield for the few steps to her own cabin. Inside, she quickly pulled on a pair of shorts and a T-shirt. Choosing to leave her feet bare, she set out for the stairs leading into the belly of the ship.

It was huge by most standards, but in the grand scheme of things it was only so big. It didn't take her long to wind her way back to the server room Jameson had shown her the first day aboard.

Reaching for the handle, Kinley wasn't surprised to find it locked. And while she did have the skills to pick it, she didn't have the tools necessary on the ship.

A spurt of frustration shot through her system.

Sagging against the wall, she rubbed the heels of her palms against her eyes. *Think*.

Jameson would have a laptop, a tablet, something he could easily access. Dammit, why hadn't she thought about that and searched his cabin? Although that might have been living life a little too close to the edge with him sleeping right there.

Okay, so she'd search the rest of the ship now and if she didn't find anything, would make it her mission to get into his stateroom again tomorrow. Alone.

She'd start on this level and work her way below. Maybe she'd get lucky and find something, if not Jameson's laptop, maybe one of the crew had one.

The ship looked completely different at night. No sunlight or strategically placed lights illuminated the small rooms. She hadn't realized just how few windows were on the ship until everything around her was pitch-black. Her fingers and hands became her guides as she felt her way down the hallways.

The eerie silence seemed to roar in her ears, along with the swish of her blood as it pumped through her veins. A loud metallic sound suddenly echoed through the hall, making her jump and gasp. *What the heck was that?*

Flattening against the wall, Kinley inched her way forward until she rounded a corner. Farther down, a rectangle of light spilled out from an open doorway. More sounds, voices, grinding and metallic clanks flowed out.

Creeping slowly, Kinley waited, pressed against the wall as she listened. A gruff, gravelly voice filled with frustration floated out to her. "I'm telling you that's not going to fix the problem."

Exasperation followed from a second voice, "I don't care. Try it anyway. At this point, we have nothing to lose. Mr. Neally indicated that we needed to get the *Queen* running as soon as possible."

"Whatever," the first voice grumbled.

Taking several deep, calming breaths, Kinley pushed against the wall as she leaned around the jamb to take a quick peek.

Two men, one of them the captain, stared at a huge piece of machinery in the middle of the room. It took her several seconds to realize the other man was on his knees, a huge wrench in his hand.

As she watched, he dropped flat to the floor and wedged beneath whatever it was they were looking at. With a frown, he reemerged. "See, I told you that wouldn't work."

Eric shrugged and started to move. Kinley jerked back and quietly darted down the hallway.

Maybe her suspicions that the *Queen* didn't really have a mechanical failure were unfounded and they were legitimately stranded.

Kinley wasn't sure how she felt about that. A little more concerned than she'd been before. It wasn't like they were sinking, but being stuck in the middle of nowhere didn't exactly give her the warm fuzzies.

And maybe, just maybe, she'd misjudged Jameson, too. Which, after tonight, she wasn't entirely certain what to do with. Did it change anything?

Probably not.

He might not be lying to her about the ship, but he'd been dishonest about plenty of other things. And he'd taken her safety net, left her vulnerable and alone.

Although she'd already been alone.

Learning that the *Queen* might actually be broken-down didn't change anything else, though. She still needed to get her hands on a computer. Sitting idly by while Jameson tried to find *her* money…that wasn't going to work for her anymore.

Propped up against the headboard, Jameson watched the picture on the monitor in front of him. The glow of the screen was the only light in the room.

It was one thing to think she might have been using sex as a distraction, but it was another to see the clear evidence of it. Oh, he wasn't surprised, but there was a definite part of him nursing some wounded pride.

It wasn't the first time in his life that he'd been used, although for some reason it hurt more. More than he'd expected it would.

The ding of an email hitting the cloning program had him jumping from one screen to another. Opening the message, his irritation mixed with pure anger and worry. The email was short, but crystal clear.

Return the money within forty-eight hours. We know where you are. With a picture of her stepping onto a plane, no doubt on her way to Tampa.

Goddammit. He shouldn't be surprised, but there was a part of him hoping that he'd overreacted to the entire situation. The email—sent to Kinley's personal, private account—suggested otherwise.

On the bright side, maybe he'd be able to trace the message and get somewhere. And even if they knew she was in Tampa, it wasn't likely someone would be able to follow them in this open expanse of water. Not without the crew noticing.

Flipping back to the video monitoring program, he watched as Kinley skulked around the ship, switching from camera to camera as she moved quietly through the space. The minute she'd slipped from his bed he'd notified Eric that she was out and about and instructed him and the staff to stay out of her way, but keep an eye on her.

He wanted to surveil her plan. What exactly was she after?

Eric, smart man that he was, had taken it a step further and used the opportunity to cement the ruse that the *Queen* was broken-down. He'd have to congratulate his captain on the play.

She moved at will, clearly searching through the ship for something. He could only assume she wanted a computer considering her hesitation outside the work space she'd seen when they'd boarded.

Hell, he half expected to watch her pry open the lock. Not that it would have done her much good considering he'd secured everything inside. Just in case.

At least the search had kept her busy. Jameson was just about to close the lid on the laptop and call it a night—the staff was also keeping an eye on her and in an hour and a half her search had been fruitless—but when he realized the direction she was heading, he hesitated.

Coming up from below deck, she moved through the salon toward the staterooms. Her cabin was farther down the hallway, tucked into a corner running alongside the galley.

Jameson held his breath when she paused just outside his door.

The picture on the screen seemed to distort and wave as he waited. Breath backed up into his lungs and he wasn't certain which he'd rather her do—come inside or keep moving.

If she came inside there wouldn't be enough time to make the laptop disappear. He also wouldn't be able to pretend that he wasn't aware she'd sneaked out of his bed after sex. It would be easier if she kept going.

But what he really wanted was for her to open the door, walk into his room and demand something from him. Argue with him. Kiss the hell out of him as she'd done earlier. Let him touch and taste her again.

It would be messy, but it would be fun. And oh so enjoyable.

Which was probably why his heart sank a little when her quiet feet carried her away.

Closing his eyes, Jameson let his head fall back as he closed the laptop.

Crap.

His entire body was tied in knots over this woman. And if he was honest with himself, had been for months. Letting his body rule hadn't been the wisest decision, but God, it had felt good.

She was lying to him and had used him. He was

lying and manipulating her. Not a great foundation for anything, especially trust.

He wanted her more now than he ever had before. Kinley Sullivan was frustrating, complicated and enticing. Her story was twisted in ways that made him ache for her even as he worried she'd never be able to find her way out of the tangled mess of a corner she'd backed herself into. She knowingly antagonized dangerous people because she could. Because it was the right thing to do.

And while his own moral compass might occasionally get rusty, he appreciated what she did and the sacrifices she'd made to use her skills for good.

Because he did the same, even if no one in their world knew it. Hell, his cover for FBI and Homeland was so well-structured even Anderson Stone had had a difficult time connecting the dots.

He knew exactly why she did the things she did. His path to working for the good guys might have been a little less straightforward, but he'd still made it.

One thing was certain: Kinley never made things easy. But he supposed easy was often boring.

With a groan, he set the computer on the bedside table and tried to relax so he could fall asleep. When that didn't work, he pushed up from the bed, gathered the clothes he'd discarded all over the cabin in his haste to have her and put them on.

This time, he was the one slipping quietly out the cabin door to roam the decks like a silent wraith.

Only he wasn't searching. He didn't have to, considering he knew exactly where to find what he wanted.

In her own cabin.

She'd slept for shit. A combination of vivid, spicy dreams of Jameson kissing her, loving her, making her body hum with pleasure mixed with haunting memories and flashes of her worst nightmares. Experiences from her childhood that she'd thought were long forgotten.

The night she'd fled Vegas, scared and alone, certain her father's men would find her before she made it to safety. Another night filled with warm, Caribbean heat and bullets popping against the trunks of trees beside her as she fled from a Russian mobster she'd pissed off.

Panic and desire did not play well together.

Her body was a mixture of physically exhausted and mentally charged. Her fight-or-flight instinct was in overdrive, but there was nowhere to go and nothing to fight.

Except Joker.

Which was probably why she was grumpy and less than polite when he walked into the salon where the staff had set out a buffet for breakfast.

Goddamn him for looking amazing while she felt like death warmed over. Her eyes were scratchy, her skin felt tight, and a dull ache pounded just behind her temples. While he shared a bright smile with the girl who'd just refilled the pitcher of cranberry juice.

"Aren't you a ray of sunshine," she grumbled, her voice spreading doom and gloom instead.

Cutting her a sideways glance, Jameson snagged a plate and filled it from the domed serving platters set along the sideboard. "And why wouldn't I be?" Pausing beside her, he leaned into her personal space. His breath brushed against her cheek and the unencumbered strands of his hair tickled her neck. "That's what happens when I have sex with a gorgeous woman."

Her body responded to his words in a way that was pure torture…because she didn't plan to do anything about the tingling awareness crackling beneath her skin.

But that didn't mean she couldn't give him a nice big dose of his own medicine. She was strong enough to play the game without putting herself in jeopardy. Wasn't she?

Turning, she let her breasts brush against the hard plane of his chest. "At least one of us is satisfied after last night," she murmured, a perfect, needling smile tugging at her lips.

His entire face went slack with shock. Kinley's grin only widened. There was something so satisfying about setting this man on his heels.

From what she'd seen, very little bobbled his confidence and calm demeanor. So far, nothing much had ruffled his feathers and there was a power in knowing she could do it.

Even if she had to tell a lie to get there.

Unfortunately for her, it didn't take him long to find his mental footing again.

Realizing she needed to get out of Dodge, Kinley moved to scoot around him, but before she could escape Jameson wrapped an arm around her waist. He pulled her tight against the long, lean length of his body.

Her own remembered the feel of him, responding immediately. The spot between her thighs hummed and heated. Anticipation and energy raced through her system. He could reach down and kiss her. Hell, she could go up on her toes and take what she wanted.

Neither of them moved in that direction.

Instead, Jameson stared, those gorgeous green eyes boring into her. Suddenly Kinley felt...uncomfortable. Caught. Like she needed to escape.

It wasn't just that he held her. It was that he saw her. More than she'd ever let anyone see. More than she wanted him to know.

Kinley tried to look away, but her body wouldn't respond to the danger signal blaring through her brain. Mesmerized and caught, she simply stood there, waiting, breath backed into her lungs and body on fire.

Finally, his lips quirked into a knowing grin as he leaned in. Jameson's words were quiet, even as she felt like they echoed loudly through the entire room. "We both know that's a lie, *cucciola*. I'll never forget the expression of ecstasy on your face. Or the way your body trembled against mine." His voice dropped even lower. "Or the feel of your orgasm as you clenched tight around my throbbing cock."

Damn. She was not prepared for that. His silky words might as well have been a tempting stroke of hand along her skin. Kinley felt like he'd touched her. All over. At once.

This game was not stacked in her favor. And if there was one lesson she'd learned from her father, it was to recognize when to cut bait and run.

Pushing against his chest, Kinley forced some space between them. Pulling in a deep breath, she kept her voice steady as she lied through her teeth. "If it makes you feel better, keep telling yourself that, cowboy."

Seven

Jameson tried to keep the smirk off his face as he watched Kinley hightail it out of the salon. He wasn't even sure she remembered the plate of food she clutched in her hand, although maybe she planned to eat breakfast on the sundeck.

God, he enjoyed sparring with that woman. A little too much.

He stood there, debating the merits of letting her go versus following behind her and keeping the pressure on. But the beat of music from his phone stopped him. And the specific song killed any remaining heat that bubbled through his blood.

Hell, he really didn't want to take this call. But it would be worse if he didn't.

Snagging the phone from his pocket, Jameson hit the big green button. "Joker."

"Man, where are you?"

Joker set his plate aside, any appetite he might have had vanishing. He didn't have many, so he really hated lying to his friends. And even though they lived in different cities and rarely saw each other, Jameson considered Gray Lockwood a friend. So this was about to suck.

"Home."

"Huh." The single sound echoed on the line, piercing him right in the belly. "That's weird because I'm outside your place right now and you're clearly not answering your door."

Shit, shit, shit.

Out of the corner of his eye, Joker watched Kinley march into the salon and grab a set of silverware off the gleaming mahogany table. She speared him with a glare, tossed her long, gorgeous hair over her shoulder and marched out.

Like he needed the reminder of the ass he was currently being to his friend and her brother.

"Fine, I'm not home." Joker reminded himself that he didn't owe Gray an explanation of his whereabouts. "What can I do for you?"

"Oh, nothing. I was in town and thought I'd stop by so we could grab some lunch."

"Why are you in Tampa?" The question was out of Joker's mouth before he realized that his friend didn't owe him an explanation of his movements either.

"I came to see you."

"You came from Charleston just to see me?" Why would his friend do that? Sure, occasionally Joker traveled to Charleston—home base for Stone Surveillance—for a specific case or to meet with the rest of the guys. He couldn't think of a single time when Gray Lockwood had hopped a plane to fly down and see him.

Not that it would be difficult considering Anderson Stone provided his team with access to the family jet whenever they wanted. The point was, his friend had never availed himself of the perk before.

Why now? When his sister was currently hiding out on Joker's yacht? Joker's eyes narrowed. Something about this didn't add up.

"We have a new client in the area and I thought I'd kill two birds with one stone."

Letting out the breath he hadn't realized he'd been holding, Joker's body sagged against the sideboard. "Well then, I'm sorry I missed you. I'm playing a bit of hooky on the *Queen*."

"Ahh, well that explains it. Enjoy the open water and I'll talk to you whenever you get back to dry land."

"Great, man. Let me know if you need any assistance with the new client."

"I'm good but appreciate the offer."

The line went dead. Joker listened to the sudden silence for several seconds before dropping the phone from his ear.

Something about the phone call had left an uneasy feeling in the pit of his stomach. Maybe it was just guilt.

The smart play here would be to go below deck and bury his nose in a computer. But so far, he hadn't gotten anywhere in finding whoever had taken Kinley's money. Not to mention, he had several programs running to track the transaction and figure out where the funds had disappeared to.

What he needed to do was work a different angle and question Kinley, something he'd been putting off. He needed to get a better idea of who might want to steal from her. Who her last few targets were.

Something told him she wasn't likely to be cooperative this morning. Which meant he needed to use a little finesse.

Clearly, Jameson wanted something from her. Something that didn't involve taking her clothes off. They'd been on the sundeck for a couple hours and the longer they were together the more restless Kinley became.

Jameson was being nice. Talking to her. Asking questions, which also made her wary. But so far all he'd done was chitchat. The kind of conversation you'd have with a stranger you met in a bar and wanted to get to know better.

But they didn't have that kind of relationship and were far from some random meet.

No doubt, he knew just as much about her as she already knew about him. So the questions he asked were all for show. To lull her into a false sense of… security? Familiarity? Trust?

Not that it really mattered. She wasn't falling for it.

What bothered her almost as much—even if she didn't want to admit it—was that Jameson hadn't made a single move all morning. Hell, he hadn't so much as accidentally brushed a hand against her or offered to apply her sunscreen.

Who would have thought that *not* touching her could drive her just as crazy as having him all over her? Her body remembered and wanted. Having him close was sending her brain into overdrive and frying her circuits.

She had a few choices. She could confront him outright to force his hand. Make him admit what he wanted from her. Probably the smartest idea, but hardly the most fun. She could attempt to torment him, just as she'd done the other day. But considering she'd already played that hand, probably not the best choice either.

Maybe she should play the same game, get him to relax and open up to her instead of the other way around.

Slipping her sunglasses down, Kinley turned to look at Jameson. Stretched out on a lounger about five feet away, his golden skin glowed in the sunlight. No man who spent all his time in a basement in front of a computer should look like that.

"I'm bored." Kinley purposely put a little edge of whine in the words. "Give me a computer."

A single eyebrow lifted. "No."

Kinley growled as she collapsed against her chair. "Seriously, Jameson. I can't sit here doing nothing. At least let me look at my email."

He gave her the side-eye but kept silent. Kinley thought he'd ignore her, so was surprised when he surged up from his chair.

Two strides had him crossing the space between them. His tall body loomed over her, blocking the sun and casting a cool shadow. Her heart fluttered; she wasn't sure if it was anticipation or apprehension. Maybe a little of both.

Silently, Jameson held out a hand. When she hesitated he said, "Come on."

"Why?"

His only answer was to shake his head. Slowly, Kinley grasped his hand. Jameson pulled, lifting her up out of the chair like it was nothing.

She expected him to let go, but instead, he used their connection to lead her through the ship. They went down the tiny, winding stairs to the very bottom deck and a door she hadn't noticed before. Not even during her midnight exploration.

Kinley was shocked when it opened into a vast room with a platform, two Jet Skis and a view of the bright blue ocean stretched before them.

Jet Skis? There were Jet Skis?

Kinley swung an accusing glance his way. "You told me we were trapped on the ship until the part arrives." The consternation in her voice wasn't contrived, she truly felt betrayed.

Jameson's mouth twisted into a playful grin. "We are."

Kinley spread her arm wide silently indicating the two huge machines in front of them.

"They don't have enough range to get us to the mainland. They're great for some fun, but nothing more."

Kinley's eyes narrowed. Was he telling her the truth? It wasn't like she knew much about Jet Skis. She'd never been on one before. Standing next to them, they seemed huge. But they were actually much smaller than a tiny boat and likely didn't have a large gas tank. He probably was telling the truth.

Reaching behind her, Jameson hit a button and a mechanical whir echoed through the chamber. The Jet Skis started to move and she realized he'd activated the crane that would lift them into the water.

Opening a closet, he pulled out two life jackets. Instead of handing her one—what she'd expected— he wrapped an arm around her waist and pulled her closer.

The wide expanse of his shoulders and chest blocked out everything but him. She could smell a combination of sunscreen and male, somehow tropical and tempting.

He was so close. And it took everything inside her not to lean forward to touch her mouth to his skin.

Grasping her arms, he slid both into the holes of the jacket. The backs of his fingers caressed her chest as he secured the three buckles that ran down the front. It wasn't until he was done, the straps pulled tight so the jacket fit snugly, before her brain functioned enough to look up and say, "I can do that myself."

And if her words hadn't come out low and husky, maybe they would have both believed them.

"I'm fully aware that you can take care of yourself, Kinley. You've been doing it for a very long time. But sometimes, every now and again, it's nice to let someone do something for you."

Somehow, she didn't think he was talking about fastening her life jacket.

A lump formed in her throat and unexpectedly, something sharp prickled the backs of her eyes. "I can't do that."

His fingers brushed against her cheek as he tucked a single strand of hair behind her ear. "You can. You can let people into your life, Kinley. Not everyone is out to hurt you."

She shook her head. "Says the man who stole from me, manipulated me and has kidnapped me onto a yacht."

"To protect you."

"You don't know me well enough to care about protecting me."

It was his turn to shake his head. "You're wrong. There are people who want you safe. People who want to love and protect you. Care about you. Get to know you."

How did he know exactly what to say to seduce her? "Even the devil uses temptation to convince you to sin."

Jameson stared at her, those green eyes clear and bright. "I'm no devil, Kinley."

It was her turn to twist her mouth into a grin. "That's what the devil would say, Jameson."

She needed to stop this conversation right now. Luckily, the Jet Skis hit the water with a quiet splash, offering the perfect distraction.

Jameson had no idea why he'd said those things to Kinley. Sure, it was in his best interest for her to trust him, but it wasn't likely given the circumstances.

No, there'd been something in her expression... something vulnerable, and he'd felt the need to reassure her.

Although now she'd pulled away from him. Maybe a little diversion on the Jet Skis would work in his favor.

"Have you ever ridden before?"

Kinley shook her head. "Nope."

He went over the controls for the machine, a couple of safety things because her brother would kill him if she got injured on his watch, and then helped her get on.

"Wait until I get on mine and we'll go out together." Turning away, Jameson reached for his own life jacket, but before one arm was even inside, he heard the roar of the Jet Ski engine as she took off.

"Son of a..."

Snapping just the first buckle, Jameson vaulted onto his own Jet Ski, punched it and ripped out into the open water.

He shouldn't have been surprised to see Kinley

bobbing and weaving as she maneuvered through the water with ease. That woman could do anything.

She was fearless, which was both alarming and arousing at the same time.

Giving it everything he had, Jameson tried to catch up. Looking behind her, Kinley tossed him the widest, most challenging grin he'd ever seen. A clear *come and get me* signal that he had no intention of ignoring.

When he got his hands on her...

They crisscrossed the water, sending giant plumes of spray up behind them.

"Slow down!" Jameson yelled, but she either ignored him or didn't hear. If he had to guess, it was the first.

The roaring sound of her laughter lifted above everything else. Well, at least she was having a good time.

Finally, after about fifteen minutes of playing catch me if you can, Kinley throttled down the Jet Ski and slid to a stop in the water. Waves rippled out around her and his own Jet Ski dipped when he screamed to a halt beside her.

"What were you thinking?"

She shrugged. "That it looked like fun and I was ready to go."

He wanted to throttle her.

"Loosen up, Jameson. Have some fun."

Fun? She wanted fun? Fine. With a flick of his wrist, Jameson sent his own Jet Ski leaping forward... and a plume of water straight over her.

He heard her yell as he pulled away. "You'll pay for that!"

Standing up, Jameson gripped the handles as he twisted backward for a look. Even drenched she looked gorgeous. Water dripped from her face. Rivulets ran down her long, tanned body, glistening in the sun.

The surprise didn't hold her captive long, though. Within seconds of him spraying her, Kinley had her own Jet Ski barreling after him. It was his turn to laugh as the wind and spray coated his skin.

Clearly, Kinley could handle herself so he'd stop worrying. Taking a deep breath, Jameson closed his eyes and let the exhilaration flow through him. Adrenaline pumped into his blood. The whine of the engine filled his head just as the echo of the vibration rumbled beneath his skin.

Power. The feeling of it was intoxicating and addictive.

But maybe shutting his eyes wasn't the smartest move because when he opened them Kinley was pacing neck and neck with him. Damn, she was fast. He had the thing wide open since there were no obstacles or threats anywhere nearby.

Leaning forward, he pushed all the speed he could get and barely leaped forward an inch. Kinley did the same, surging ahead. But there must have been something neither of them had seen floating near the surface of the water because one minute she was beside him, the next, the nose of her Jet Ski was barreling straight for him.

He watched it happen, but it was so fast there was nothing he could do to stop it. They were racing, and then water surrounded him.

Eight

Kinley had no time to react. The water was smooth beneath her Jet Ski as she raced forward, and then it wasn't. Suddenly something dark floated in front of her, just beneath the surface. An animal. A log. She wasn't sure. But there was no time to avoid it. The bump bucked her off the seat, the steering jerked, and her machine headed straight on a collision course with Jameson.

She tried to wrench the handles in the opposite direction, but nothing happened. The loud sound of plastic and metal colliding slammed against her eardrums just as her entire body plunged into the water.

Her lungs didn't have time to prepare. Her mouth was open, a warning yell streaming out. Salt water entered her throat and burned her nose. Her body reacted on instinct, kicking for the surface even though she didn't know which way was up.

But her life jacket did. Seconds after plunging beneath the surface, her body popped free. Kinley sputtered and coughed even as her lungs struggled to inflate with air. Disoriented, she tried to clear the water from her eyes and take stock—of her own body and everything around her.

Jameson. It was the first clear thought. Her mouth opened to yell his name, but her lungs weren't clear enough and the only sound that came out was a mangled croak.

Her ears worked fine though as her own name bounced off the surface of the water. "Kinley!" Even dazed, she could hear the utter panic in the single word.

He wasn't just scared for her. He was terrified. Did people who didn't care about you get terrified when you were in trouble?

Kinley wouldn't know. She'd never really had anyone who cared about her.

Her left elbow smarted, her left shin burned and there was likely a huge bump on her forehead based on the ache centered there. But for the most part, she was fine. "I'm okay," she finally managed to say, even if the words weren't as loud as she wanted them to be.

About twenty feet in front of her, the Jet Ski she'd been driving bobbed quietly in the water. The safety must have kicked in and the engine had turned off the minute she'd fallen.

Something strong grabbed her life jacket and

hauled her several feet through the water. Her body spun until she stared into Jameson's face. His expression was dark and desperate. Beneath the water, his hands ran over her limbs as far as he could reach.

Why hadn't he touched her like that before, on the deck?

"Are you okay?"

She didn't answer his question, mostly because she wasn't entirely certain of the answer. "I'm sorry."

He shook her, gently, her body moving in the water. "Are you hurt?"

"No. A little. Maybe. Are you okay?"

His eyes squeezed shut for several seconds. When they opened again, some of the overwhelming panic that had filled his expression eased. "Explain to me, please."

"Answer my question first."

"I'm fine. You?"

"My elbow hurts, but it's just a bump. My lower leg burns so I assume I have a scrape but since I don't see blood in the water, it probably isn't bad. And my forehead aches, but I'm not dizzy, seeing double or nauseous, so most likely just a bump."

Jameson blinked at her, bobbing in the water. His hands curled into the upper edges of her life jacket and hauled her out of the water until her chest collided with his. The wind knocked out of her lungs, again, just as his mouth found hers.

Kinley's world spun, but this time that had nothing to do with a physical change to her orientation. It was all Jameson.

The kiss held an edge of desperation that she felt

deep in the center of her soul. She recognized it. Returned it. Needed more. Her lungs burned, but she didn't care. Tilting her head, she let her own mouth make demands of his. Her tongue darted out, tangling with Jameson's.

He tasted of salt and sun and sin.

But before she could coordinate her body to take more, Jameson let her go. Her body, buoyed by the life jacket, bobbed in the water.

"You scared the shit out of me, Kinley."

She blinked, somehow finding the brain power to reply. "Clearly."

But she had no idea what to do with that information.

Glancing around, Jameson swore softly. "Can you ride back?"

For the first time, Kinley looked about and realized she, Jameson and the two Jet Skis floating nearby were the only things in sight. She could no longer see the *Queen* and a sudden spurt of panic mixed with the adrenaline still pumping through her system.

"Yes." Kinley wasn't positive of the answer, but it was really the only option. She'd make it back, one way or another.

Jameson stared at her for several seconds before saying, "Stay here."

With powerful strokes, he headed out to the Jet Ski she'd been driving. As he hauled himself up onto the machine, Kinley did *not* stare at the powerful rope of muscles across his shoulders and arms.

In no time he had the engine roaring, but he barely pushed it past idle as he drove it close. Holding out his hand to her, he used their connections to hoist her out of the water and onto the seat behind him. Instinct had her wrapping her arms around his waist.

Peering over his shoulder, Jameson asked again, "Are you sure you can drive?"

What were their choices? He could drive them both to the yacht, leaving behind one of the Jet Skis to probably never be seen again, or she could suck it up and get herself back to the ship. Taking stock one more time, Kinley realized all of her injuries were superficial.

"I'm fine."

Jameson's only response was a quick nod before he launched himself off the Jet Ski. His long, lean body stretched into a perfect dive. His hands above his head cut through the water with barely a silent splash. Even with the life jacket, he didn't surface for several seconds, and when he did he was halfway to his own Jet Ski.

She watched as he pulled himself out of the water once more. Flipping his machine around, he brought it even with hers.

"We're going to take this nice and slow." His eyes narrowed as he silently waited for her agreement. Clearly, this wasn't the time to showboat or argue, so she nodded.

Taking her at her word, Jameson headed back in the direction they'd come. Or at least Kinley assumed that's where they were headed, since during her crash and plunge, she'd lost all orientation. And without any landmarks...

Jameson kept the Jet Skis at a low, respectable speed. The vibration running through the machine and into her amped up the ache in her forehead, but she wasn't about to complain. Her body felt stiff and her injuries smarted. What had felt like a five-minute ride out morphed into an eternity on the way back.

Kinley let out a breath she hadn't realized she'd been holding when the *Queen* finally came into focus. Now she could admit to the silent fear that they'd be lost in the Gulf, all alone.

She really had been an idiot.

Two of the staff were waiting on the rear deck of the yacht as they pulled up next to the ship. With a few quick words, Jameson turned the Jet Skis over to them.

He waved away a young man, the guy she'd seen with Eric the other night, who tried to help her up out of the water. Jameson's eyebrows crinkled together as he lifted her onto the deck himself.

She expected him to let her go, so she was surprised when he didn't. Jameson reached for the buckles on her life jacket and with quick, sure motions popped them all free. He let the jacket fall to the deck with a wet plop.

Kinley was stunned when he dropped into a crouch on the deck in front of her. Instinct had her hands shooting out to touch his shoulders for balance.

The warmth of his skin melted through her fingers even as his own skimmed purposely over her legs. He was checking for injuries. Logically, her brain knew it. But the rest of her body simply responded to his touch.

The soft, gentle brush of his hands. Breath backed into her lungs when his fingertips grazed the top of her inner thighs. Her hold on him tightened even as her body unconsciously leaned into his touch.

His exploration was quick and thorough. Jameson surged up off the deck even as his hands skimmed her hips, waist, arms and chest, sending prickling awareness snapping beneath her skin.

Wrapping one hand against the nape of her neck, Jameson threaded his fingers through the wet strands of her hair. Using his hold, he urged her head backward.

The man loomed above her, and if it had been anyone else, no doubt she might have felt uneasy or trapped. But with him, she felt…hyper aware. Of how close he was. The way he held her, gentle yet commanding.

His other hand brushed softly against her forehead, pressing carefully. Kinley winced when he hit a tender spot.

"You definitely have a bump."

She could have told him that. "I'm fine." Maybe her words would have carried more weight if she'd pulled away from his inspection instead of leaning into it like a sunflower searching for light.

"Seeing double? Feeling nauseous?"

Kinley shook her head, and then immediately regretted the movement. "No."

Grasping his hand, Kinley extricated herself from

his hold. It was either that or embarrass herself in front of the staff as she jumped his bones.

"I'm fine," Kinley said again, squeezing his hand before she let it drop. "I'm really sorry. I wasn't thinking about how dangerous it could be, out there with nothing and no one around."

She expected a lecture, an *I told you so*, something. Instead, Jameson's only response was, "I'm very happy you're okay."

The way he watched her, those sharp, intelligent eyes taking in everything, made her feel both seen and protected. Two things that also made her completely uneasy because they were so unfamiliar.

This was quickly getting out of hand. She was getting out of hand.

"I'm going to lie down." What she wanted was escape, from him, and if she was honest, from the whirling thoughts in her own brain.

She'd taken several steps when she realized Jameson was right behind her. She didn't think anything of it, until instead of continuing down the hallway to his own stateroom, he stopped just outside hers.

There was room to pass her, so clearly, he was waiting for something.

"I'm fine," she said once more.

"If you say so. But you might have a concussion, so until we're sure you don't, you can't be alone."

If his own emotions weren't a tangled mess he might have appreciated the utter expression of dismay on Kinley's face. But as it was, her clear torture was nothing compared to his own.

Jameson's hands curled into fists at his side. It was either that or reach for her. Not only did he want to reassure himself—again—that she was uninjured, but he wanted the feel of her warm, silky skin against his fingertips.

The reel of her accident kept rolling through his head, with a different, unhappy ending. One that resembled the aftermath of the accident that had killed his parents when he was eleven.

No, it wasn't the same, but for some reason, Kinley's accident had triggered those difficult memories.

He wanted to snag her and kiss the hell out of her, for reassurance and to block out the images. He wanted the moans of her pleasure ringing in his ears and the caress of her panting breaths as she lost all ability to speak because he was driving her body to heights of pleasure.

Unfortunately, there was also a part of him that wanted to shake some sense into her and yell because she'd been so reckless with her own safety. Their safety.

Together, those things did not mix well. His emotions were churning close to the surface and his hold on them was tenuous at best. But he also recognized that given the sizable lump on her forehead, Kinley couldn't be alone.

And while he could ask one of the staff to watch her, he didn't trust them to keep as close a watch for signs of concern as he would. There was also a huge part of him, after the utter fear of watching the accident in slow motion and the way she'd disappeared beneath the water, that wasn't ready to let her out of his sight.

So they were stuck with each other. For a little while.

"No." Kinley's single word was emphatic...almost desperate.

"Yes."

Folding her arms across her chest, she asked, "Remind me, when did you get your medical degree?"

They both knew that was a rhetorical question. "Look, you shouldn't be alone, at least for a couple hours. You have two choices. You can let me into your room or we can go above deck."

She blinked at him. Her fist, tight around the handle to the door of her stateroom, flexed. He knew her well enough to understand the calculation going on behind those gorgeous blue eyes of hers.

"Feel free to try to beat me into the room and lock me out. But the staff have a universal key and can open every door. Don't think I won't use it."

"This isn't a good idea."

On that, they agreed. He really hoped she didn't choose her room because his honor was hanging by a thread. But he did still have some pride. And while, sure, they'd already slept together once, clearly Kinley had used sex as a weapon of distraction. She'd sneaked away from his room in the middle of the night—to snoop—and she hadn't come back.

None of her actions since then had indicated she actually wanted him to touch her. Oh, sure, she'd responded to the kiss out in the water, but that was pure survival and relief.

"Your choice," he reiterated.

Sighing, Kinley said, "At least give me a few minutes to change my clothes."

Since he did have a key and could get into her room any time he wanted—not that he'd use it without good reason—Jameson agreed. "Ten minutes. If you're not up on deck I'm coming to get you."

Giving him a jaunty salute, Kinley tossed him a grimace as she disappeared into her suite.

Jameson used the time to change his own clothes. He took stock and bandaged the cut on his own thigh. He hadn't even realized it was there until he'd climbed back onto the *Queen*. No doubt adrenaline had masked the burn of the salt water.

Purposely choosing board shorts that covered the injury, he tossed on a light green button-down shirt and a pair of deck shoes. He didn't bother with much of anything else before padding up to the sun deck.

It was late enough in the day that the sun had begun to sink slowly in the horizon. Beautiful colors painted the sky—purple, red, pink and orange. Pale enough to match the calm sea around them. A breeze kicked up, teasing the edges of the shirt he'd left untucked.

He was standing at the railing, looking out into the vast expanse of nothing, when she sidled up beside him. Flipping his wrist over, he glanced at the watch resting there. "One minute to spare."

"I figured I'd pressed my luck enough today."

He couldn't help the slight smile that tugged at his lips. "Probably right."

It had been a day. It certainly didn't feel like he'd woken up in his bed alone after a night of unbelievable pleasure with the woman beside him. But for some reason, standing there with her, everything but an unexpected peace melted away.

They stood, silent, together, as the sun disappeared.

And when it was finished, Kinley turned from the water. Stretching her arms out along the railing behind her, she lifted her gaze to his.

"Now what?"

If only he knew.

Nine

She needed a distraction. Something to break the quiet comfort of the moment they'd just shared.

She didn't do shared moments, although it was getting more and more difficult to remember that with this man.

Kinley wasn't down for a candlelit dinner in the salon. Romance was the last thing she was looking for. In her earlier search of the ship she'd found a cabinet with several games—chess, checkers, some random childhood classics. And a deck of cards.

"How about a game?" Because she needed something else to concentrate on besides what her body wanted her to do with Jameson.

His eyebrow quirked up, question and intrigue. "What kind of game?"

"Poker." Wait, maybe this was a great idea. One she could turn in her favor. "And how about to make things interesting we add a friendly wager."

A small smile tugged at the corner of Jameson's lips. "How friendly? What game?"

"Strip poker?" Even as she was certain her clothes were safely staying on her body, a little flutter of expectation tickled her chest.

"I'm underdressed for that game."

"Oh, so you don't think you can beat me? Surely a man with your brains and brilliance can play a little poker."

The smirk on his lips twisted into a full-blown smile. "Fine. We'll play."

The sensation of triumph was short-lived when Jameson walked over to a cabinet built into a seat that ran the length of the deck. Indicating the table she'd used the other day for breakfast, he didn't wait for her to sit before popping open the box and spilling the deck into his palm.

With quick, dexterous fingers, he began shuffling the cards. Oh, not just a normal, run-of-the-mill bridge. Nope, he had the deck waterfalling from one hand to the other, cards being cut and spun out of the deck before rejoining the stack. Clearly, the man was also a magician.

But he wasn't the only one with a few tricks up his sleeves.

"Impressive," Kinley said as she sat across from him. Night was firmly settling in and the stars began popping out against the inky sky. Kinley had to admit that without the distraction of blinding lights, they seemed so bright. Bigger than life. And made her realize just how small she was in the universe.

But that wasn't her focus right now. Beating this man and winning was.

"Texas Hold'em?" Jameson asked as he continued to make the deck sing in his hands.

"Sure." Everyone knew Texas Hold'em. The game had been around a long time, but thanks to some publicity several years ago had found its way into mainstream culture. Which was why Kinley wasn't surprised when he suggested it.

The game consisted of dealing each player two cards—the hole cards. The first three cards—known as the flop—were faceup on the table, available to every player. Rounds of betting happened before the display of the community cards and then again with the fourth—the turn—and the fifth card, known as the river.

But for their purposes, betting wouldn't be necessary.

Two cards came sliding across the table in front of her. Laying a palm on top, Kinley peeled up just the corners before dropping them. An eight and a ten, unsuited. Not a great hand, but not a terrible one either.

If they'd been playing for money, she might have used their first few hands to gauge him as a player or bully him out of a pot. And, sure, they could still fold, but in this game that meant defeat and losing an article of clothing, so it wouldn't really matter.

Jameson turned up the first three cards, tossing out

the queen of spades, the seven of diamonds and the ten of spades. She'd pulled a pair. He paused before rolling another card, the eight of spades. Two pair. And then the king of clubs.

Jameson's gaze ran across the cards on the table. He pulled up the corner of his own hold cards and then studied her for several seconds. "Roll them."

Kinley felt pretty confident, right up until Jameson turned over the jack and nine of spades. "Flush."

She didn't even bother showing her cards but tossed them into the pile in the center of the table. Reaching down, she pulled off the sandal on her right foot and added it.

Everything inside her wanted to wipe the satisfied smirk off Jameson's face. And she wasn't above cheating…she simply needed to get her hands on the deck in order to do it.

Her brain was spinning on what argument she could use when he provided her the perfect opportunity.

"This would be more interesting if the stakes were higher."

A thrill of adrenaline shot through her system. "Agreed. Clearly, you have a suggestion."

"Why don't we bet like we normally would…only use the number of items we're willing to lose instead of chips."

Kinley scanned Jameson's body. The warm weather didn't exactly lend itself to layers of clothing, so neither of them had a lot to wager. However, as she silently counted the articles of clothing she could see,

Kinley realized she probably had on more. And held the advantage.

"Sure, but I think the dealer should swap back and forth. And if you fold, you lose whatever you've wagered up to that point."

"Makes sense to me."

Slowly, Jameson picked her sandal up from the middle of the table. He ran his thumb slowly along the leather strap, never breaking eye contact with her the entire time. Mischief and promise smoldered deep in his eyes and for some reason Kinley's body reacted as if he was stroking her instead of her shoe.

Jerking her gaze to the table, Kinley concentrated on gathering the cards—and the shreds of her composure. She might not have the fancy shuffling skills he did, but she handled the deck with skill and efficiency.

Her father had taught her a few useful things, like how to fly under the radar and make the cards you wanted pop from the deck. He'd expected her to go undetected, which was the opposite of the showboating Jameson had done during his turn.

She'd lost the first hand; there was no way she would lose the next.

With the intention of distracting him, she casually mentioned, "My head is fine, by the way. I don't even have a headache anymore. No concussion."

His eyes narrowed. "You wouldn't be lying in order to avoid me, would you?"

Kinley grimaced. "I'm with you right now. And, no."

Slowly, Jameson nodded. "I'm glad you're feeling better."

At least she'd dodged that bullet.

Dealing herself a pair of pocket jacks, she made sure to give Jameson something equally as enticing—an ace and king. Now that they were wagering, she didn't want him to fold and take the deal back because he didn't have anything worth playing in his hand.

Before turning any cards faceup, Kinley said, "Your bet." And he fell straight into her trap by betting, "One."

Kinley pulled up the corner of her cards—as if she couldn't remember what they were—and said, "Call."

She turned three cards—the flop—an ace, a three and a seven. He didn't even wait for her to ask before saying, "One."

She also didn't hesitate. "Call."

The fourth card—the turn—didn't do either of them any good with a ten. However, that didn't stop him from betting. "One." Or her accepting by calling.

They were both up to three pieces of clothing and Kinley knew exactly which one of them would win this hand. Flipping the last card—the river—she revealed a third jack. The cards on the table were unassuming, designed to give him the impression that she might also be holding one pair with an ace in her hand, but the hope that his kicker would beat hers.

She'd dealt the hand purposely, not to give him something that left him overly confident, but also with a minor probability that she had something big in her own hand. So she was surprised when he checked instead of betting.

And rather than push her luck to the point of making him question whether the hand had been fairly dealt, she checked as well. Together, they turned their cards.

Jameson's eyes narrowed when he saw her three jacks. "Lucky river."

Kinley shrugged. "That's part of the game. I believe you owe me three."

Standing up, Jameson towered over the table. His wide shoulders blocked out the soft yellow light from the sconces on the wall and cast half of his body in shadow.

She hadn't realized just how quiet and dark it had become. How suddenly alone she felt. Alone except for the man across from her.

Bending, he slipped both shoes off his feet and deliberately placed them on the table between them. He watched her, his gaze contemplative. She was afraid those pale green eyes, so intelligent, saw right through her. She was good, but maybe he'd spotted the stacked deck somehow.

Walking around the table, Jameson grabbed the top button of his shirt and popped it free. Slowly, he circled around until he was standing just beside her. Kinley's fingers, resting on the arm of the chair, dangled inches away from his hip. Need blasted through her as she turned to stare up at him.

Her throat was dry. Kinley wanted to say something, but nothing coherent formed in her brain. Which was entirely frustrating. She forced down a swallow, hoping to relieve the scratchy sensation as he popped the rest of the buttons through their holes, one by one.

The sides of his shirt gaped open. The solid expanse of his belly was right there. She could touch him. Lean forward and run her tongue along his skin and taste the salty perfection of him.

Her grip tightened on the arms of her chair, the whine of protesting wood giving her away.

Slowly, Jameson slipped the shirt from his wide shoulders and let the piece of clothing flutter to the deck.

"My deal."

Jameson couldn't decide if he was irritated at losing most of his clothing in one hand or thrilled at the prospect of getting some of Kinley's clothes off during the next.

Probably both.

Cards in his hands, he dealt hole cards for them both. Peeling up the corners, he revealed a pair of pocket queens. "I suppose I'm all in," he said with a small shrug.

His shorts were the last thing on so this hand was all or nothing. He was working at a clear disadvantage. Something that had never bothered him before and wasn't about to now. His entire life had been a disadvantage, foster home after foster home. The person he'd been closest to betraying him when he'd needed someone most.

These odds were nothing.

Kinley, a smug grin twisting her luscious lips, gave a little shrug of her own and said, "Call."

Slowly, Jameson turned the flop and revealed a

two, king and ten, all of different suits. Nothing much helpful. Jameson flicked the corner of the next card before turning it. "Queen of hearts." Somehow it felt a little appropriate.

An ace landed last. Probably no help to either of them. It was possible she held a high pair if she had an ace or king in her hand. Jameson watched her, studying her mannerisms, trying to discern what she held.

Poker was as much a game of observation as it was of luck. Kinley might not think she had any tells, but she really did. Or maybe he was just so attuned to her right now that he noticed the smallest of details.

The last hand, when she knew that she had him over a barrel—not that he'd known it at the time— she'd tried not to show it. Her mouth had gone perfectly flat, a straight line that wasn't natural. She was careful not to let the tiny edges curl up into the smile she always carried with her. But she also didn't give in to a frown or let the ridge between her eyes wrinkle. Her expression had gone too…perfect and plastic.

A word he'd never use to describe Kinley Sullivan. She was alive, animated. She might try to blend in, but no matter what, she stood out. Tall and gorgeous, it wasn't just her physical features, but her presence. Confident, uncaring, observant and intelligent. Along with beautiful, a deadly combination.

Last hand, she'd worked hard to become a blank slate so as not to reveal her winning hand. This time, her lips curled up…a little too much. She wanted to look happy about what she held, but the expression wasn't real. It was forced.

She had nothing. Which meant he had the power position.

"How about we add a little more to sweeten the pot?"

Kinley's eyes narrowed as she looked him up and down.

This was where the skill of the game came in. He knew she held nothing. If he pushed too hard, she'd simply fold her hand and give him her shoe.

He wanted more than that. Excitement and possibility teased him. Sitting half-naked in front of her, he wanted her half-naked—no, totally exposed—as well.

He'd always been a man to gamble. Maybe not with money, but with actions. Hell, no hacker worth anything could be faint of heart. It took guts to risk what they did.

"What did you have in mind? You don't have any more clothes to offer."

She was hooked; now he had to weigh things out, offer her something she couldn't refuse. Something she wanted more than anything.

"Considering you've already seen me naked, losing my shorts really isn't going to be much of a victory, is it?"

Jameson did not miss the way her body shifted at the reminder of their night together. Uncomfortable, but not because she regretted anything. No, he could clearly see the signs of desire she tried to hide.

The peak of her nipples against the soft material of her shirt. The color staining her cheeks and running down her throat and chest. Her own arousal only served to needle his.

The physical signs she couldn't hide said she was interested in more of what they'd shared last night. But until she voiced that or showed him with purposeful action, Jameson had no intention of doing anything about it.

Desire and choice were two different things.

"No, I suppose it isn't," Kinley responded, although her words were a little unsteady. "Stop playing and just tell me the bet."

"An hour with a computer."

She didn't even hesitate. "Two."

"Agreed, in exchange for your shirt and shorts."

Kinley shook her head. "In exchange for three pieces of clothing—the one already on the table and two more—all of my choosing."

Jameson took a visual account of what she wore. She'd already lost a sandal so she had one more to match. A shirt and shorts. Whatever she was wearing beneath those. He tried not to think about that because it would cloud his judgment.

Like him, she wasn't exactly dressed for a blizzard. Either way, she'd lose a couple of strategic pieces.

"Agreed." Indicating the cards, he silently asked her to roll them, and was surprised to see a two and a ten. No wonder she'd agreed, she held two pair. Not a terrible hand, but still a risk considering the ace and king on the table.

The vein at the side of her neck pulsed with her quickened heartbeat. Jameson fought the urge to lean over and lick it. She tilted forward over the table, anticipation and adrenaline as she waited to discover her fate.

Slowly, Jameson pressed up from the table, cards still in hand. A small smirk played at the corner of his lips as he tossed his cards onto the table. "Three queens. I believe it's your turn to take a few things off."

With a groan and a grimace, Kinley plopped into her chair. "Dang it."

But she didn't protest or hesitate. Instead, she popped the buckle on her sandal before depositing it onto the table. Reaching for the hem, in one fluid motion, her shirt joined the shoe.

Had she worn that bra purposely to torment him? Pale blue lace, it was practically transparent. The swirls were strategically placed to cover her pointed nipples, but that did nothing to stop his memory of licking, tasting and sucking her breasts deep into his mouth. His tongue tingled with the need to do it all again.

Instead, he stood still and drank in the sight of her. The table between them, Kinley cocked her head as she popped the button on her white shorts. The sound of metal against metal ripped through the room as the zipper went down. She held his gaze, those bright blue eyes almost daring him, as she rolled her hips. The shorts hit the deck with a smack.

Kinley stepped backward, leaned down to scoop them up and then tossed the shorts. Not onto the table with the other things, but straight at his head.

Jameson snatched them out of the air before they

could hit him in the face. "Such a sore loser," he murmured.

Kinley crossed the deck, head high and a fierce twinkle of determination in her eyes. Gathering the cards, she didn't bother sitting as she shuffled. Her hands were quick as the cards settled onto the slick surface. Jameson glanced at his cards, seeing a ten and jack of diamonds.

He waited for the flop, a four, king of diamonds, ten. He had a pair, and a potential for a flush, although he'd played enough poker in his life to know better than to chase something with such terrible odds.

"You're already in for your shorts."

"And you're in for a bra or panties."

"Same bet as before? Your clothes and a computer against the rest of mine?"

Jameson's gaze traveled over Kinley's body. She stood, golden light spilling across her, gilding her bronzed skin. She was gorgeous. Fierce. And Jameson wanted nothing more than to take her clothes off. To enjoy exploring every inch of her delicious body once more.

But something about the way she stood, feet wide, hands relaxed at her sides, warned that he needed to move with caution. She seemed too confident.

And Jameson wasn't willing to take the chance.

Pushing his cards into the center of the table, he popped the tie on his shorts and dropped them to the deck. He hadn't bothered with anything beneath them, which she'd apparently already suspected.

With a shrug, Jameson said, "Not willing to risk that bet. You win," and plopped into his chair.

Kinley stared at him for several seconds, her eyes sharp as they toured his body. His sex responded as her gaze lingered there, hardening and lengthening beneath her watch.

The long, elegant column of her throat worked as she swallowed. The tiny point of her tongue swept out over her dark pink lips, leaving behind a trail of moisture. He wanted to follow her tongue with a swipe of his own.

Instead, he curled his hands around the arms of the chair and waited.

Ball was in her court.

And he had to admit to serious disappointment when she spun on her heel and fled from the deck.

Ten

Blood whooshed audibly in Kinley's ears. The insistent thump of it centered right between her thighs, an uncomfortable reminder of just how precarious a hold she had over her own body. Everything inside urged her to turn around, walk onto that deck and take exactly what she wanted.

And what she wanted was Jameson Neally.

But she couldn't let herself do that.

Winning should be sweet, even if she had cheated. But there was nothing sweet about this victory. Her body ached and for the life of her she couldn't remember what was important and what wasn't. Or why wanting Jameson was a bad idea.

That night, Kinley tossed and turned, plagued by vivid and difficult dreams. Her subconscious fought against her resolve, leaving her unfulfilled and on edge when she woke.

She was set for another lonely, unproductive morning of staring across an empty ocean, her mind and body unhappy with the inactivity. But Jameson had other ideas.

The sun had barely risen above the horizon when he joined her on the deck. A pleasant breeze whispered softly against her skin. The chill was enough that Kinley wished she'd grabbed a light jacket before leaving her cabin.

Hands wrapped around a cup, steam rising from the dark liquid inside, Jameson stopped beside her. His long, lean body curled over the railing. They stood together, and somehow, in the quiet stillness of the morning, Kinley found a moment of peace.

Gone was the animosity, antagonism and uncomfortable awareness that usually filled her when he was close. Taking a deep breath, she let it settle over her, accepting the gift of it for however long it lasted. Surprised to experience it with Jameson standing beside her.

Finally, after a few minutes, Jameson said, "Truce."

The single word made her lips curl into an unexpected smile.

Turning her back to the railing, her own answer was a lifted eyebrow.

"You and I have been playing games for so long I think maybe we don't know how to deal with each other not as adversaries."

It was possible he had a point, but she wasn't ready to agree that they *weren't* adversaries. "You've been tracking me for over a year, Jameson. In most circumstances that would be a crime called stalking."

He had the forethought to look chagrined, which honestly surprised her. "You're right. I'll admit to doing it because your brother asked me to keep an eye on you."

Of course he had. She still wasn't comfortable with her half brother's motives. How could he possibly forgive her for ruining his life? Hell, her actions had sent the man to prison for ten years.

"But it wasn't long before I was watching not because I needed to, but because I wanted to."

Kinley's other eyebrow joined its twin. Now that was unexpected.

"You're brilliant and a challenge. I'm damn good at what I do and I can count on one hand the number of people who can outmaneuver me."

Her burst of laughter shot between them. "Thanks. I think."

"I have the utmost respect for you, Kinley. Not only are you good at what you do, but you're a good person. And considering the life you were raised in and the life your circumstances thrust you into, not many people would choose the path you've taken."

Jameson's own laughter held an edge of self-deprecation. "I know all too well how easy it is to skirt the edge of morality. To push just a little too far into the gray until your actions become tinged with black."

Jameson might have been watching her for the past year, but she'd been watching him, too. And she was slowly realizing that she actually knew very little about him.

For some reason she wanted to understand this man. Not just the details she'd picked up because she needed to understand the man she was trying to hide from, but all the things he never shared with anyone else.

The pieces of himself he hid away.

"What do you regret, Joker?"

His body shifted. He glanced at her before pulling his gaze out to the horizon again. "I regret a lot of things."

"Like what?"

She expected him to ignore her. Or flat-out tell her no. "Early on, I trusted the wrong person, someone I looked up to. He introduced me to some friends and asked me to do some hacking work for them. Minor stuff. Erase some security footage here. Get information on people. Even back then, things I could do in my sleep."

"How old were you?"

Jameson shrugged. "Seventeen. The money was good and slowly I got pulled into bigger and bigger things. Part of it was the challenge, so it wasn't all about the money. But I'd been struggling on my own for so long, in and out of foster homes with nothing really to call my own."

"It was tempting."

His soft chuckle held no humor. "To say the least. I made decisions I'm not proud of and didn't ask the questions I should have because I convinced myself that if I didn't know the answers then what I was doing was okay.

"Until I got caught. And everyone abandoned me. Again. It shouldn't have surprised me, not by that point in my life. But for some reason it did. And it hurt."

Kinley heard the echo of the pain he must have felt and understood. Knowing the people in your life are bad doesn't stop the pain when they hurt you.

"I'm sorry. What did you do?"

This time his shrug was accompanied by a satisfied grin. "I handed law enforcement everything they needed for an open-and-shut case against a major drug dealer."

"As a plea deal?"

"Something like that."

Something told her that might have been the first time, but probably not the last, he'd helped out the good guys.

"How'd you get involved with Stone Surveillance?"

This time, his grin was wide and full of mischief. "That's a story for another time. Now, I'm starving. Let's eat."

Jameson had spent a restless night, which meant he was up early working on his tracing programs and chasing down a couple leads. By the time he joined

Kinley on the deck he'd already gotten in several hours of work trying to find her money.

He was getting desperate. And frustrated. Whoever was behind the theft and the threats against Kinley was good at hiding. Too good. Almost like they had professional help or friends in high places.

Before he'd joined Kinley, he'd been so desperate that he'd called in a few favors from a couple colleagues to see if they could run down any leads he might have missed.

Only for her would he swallow his pride.

Left with little else to do but wait, Jameson decided that spending the day with Kinley would be a good idea. Maybe she'd open up and give him some information he could use.

The day passed in a lazy, long stretch of sunshine, drinks and good conversation. When they weren't sniping at each other, Jameson realized Kinley had an unusual sense of humor. She was quick-witted and never let an opportunity to dig a little pass her by.

The more time they spent together, the more time he wanted to spend with her. Yesterday had been about distraction, but Jameson found himself asking her more and more questions. Wanting to learn about the life she'd built and who she was outside of hacking.

"Tell me you did something other than work jobs as a kid."

The sun was starting to sink behind soft white clouds. It had baked them both a little, and even if they hadn't done much, Jameson embraced the mellow energy that came from being out in the sun all day.

Apparently, so did Kinley. Surprisingly enough, she answered. A soft smile tugged at her lips and her gaze went a little hazy with memory. "No. My mom was—is—a showgirl. I remember plenty of nights sitting backstage watching the women get ready. They liked to dress me up like a little doll. Do my makeup. Put the headdresses on. From the time I was three, my mom had me in dance lessons. And I loved it."

He could hear the joy and longing in her voice.

"I'm pretty sure her plan was for me to follow in her footsteps onto the stage."

"What happened?"

Jameson wished he hadn't asked the question when her head rolled to look at him, her expression filled with the echo of pain and disappointment. "I made the mistake of letting my father know I was good with computers. He made me quit. No matter how much I begged or cajoled or bargained, he wouldn't budge. Not even my mom could convince him to let me back into classes."

"How old were you?"

Her mouth twisted into a grimace. "Twelve."

He had no doubt she'd been an amazing dancer. Even now, her long, lean body moved with a sense of innate grace.

"I'm sorry." What else could he say?

She shrugged. "Water under the bridge. But while

my life wasn't like most kids', it wasn't all terrible. I had food and a roof over my head."

"There's a lot more to life than that, Kinley."

The soft sound she made was somewhere between a huff and a laugh. "True."

He wasn't sure she actually believed that. Her life was work. She didn't let anyone close to her, and each new target consumed her. She spent her life looking over her shoulder, ready to run at the first sign of trouble.

"When was the last time you danced?"

Jameson had no idea why he'd asked the question…it had simply popped out of his mouth.

This time her laugh was genuine, if dismissive. "Oh, I don't know. Years. No, I take that back. I attended a ball in London once when I was targeting an arms dealer." The mischief in her eyes was intoxicating and enticing. Clearly, it was a good memory.

"That doesn't count. When was the last time you danced just for fun? Just for you?"

A little bit of the sparkle died in her eyes. Shaking her head, she said, "Probably when I was twelve."

Crap.

Pushing up from the lounger, Jameson crossed the deck to the stereo that had been playing softly. Up until now it had been background noise and nothing more. Flipping open the app on the tablet attached, he searched for a channel on the streaming service.

When he was happy with his selection, he bumped

up the volume so that the soft, melodic strains of music tangled with the breeze twisting across the deck.

Frank Sinatra's distinctive voice joined in, singing about the way you look tonight. Crossing the space, Jameson held out his hand.

Kinley stared, her elegant features pinched with confusion. "What are you doing?"

Surely that was obvious. "Asking you to dance."

Her gorgeous blue eyes widened, and her lush lips dropped open into a silent O. But she didn't laugh at him or the idea. Instead, slowly, she placed her hand into his.

Jameson wasn't sure who moved first, but one moment she was in the chair and the next she was standing in front of him. Staring up at him. Waiting.

Grasping her waist, he pulled her tight against his body. The feel of her…it was amazing.

They probably looked silly, gliding around the deck to music that should have been accompanied by elegant gowns and the tinkling of crystal champagne flutes. But he didn't care that she wore a tiny bikini that barely covered her rear.

In fact, he liked it because that meant he could feel the soft, velvety texture of her skin beneath his palm as he guided them both through the dance. With sure movements, Jameson spun her out into a little twirl and then pulled her close.

Her palm landed on his chest, the heat of her nearly branding him. This time, she was the one to press close and take control. The song changed, something sultry, with sizzle. Jameson's body responded, his own pulse leaping as a low, sexy voice joined in. He couldn't name the song, who sang it or even what the lyrics were.

But he felt them in every fiber of his being.

What had started out as a nice gesture was quickly turning into torture. Especially when Kinley grasped his hands, placed them on her hips and started sliding her body against his.

Using the time of the music, she dragged his hands up her body. His palms tingled where they touched her. Gone was the mischief that sparkled in her eyes, replaced by a heat he felt straight to his soul.

Somewhere, Jameson found the strength to say, "Stop."

Tilting her head, Kinley asked, "Why?"

"Because if you don't, I'm not going to be responsible for what happens next. I want you, Kinley, like I can't breathe around it."

Leaning up onto her toes, she brought her mouth a breath away from his and whispered, "Then take what you want."

Everything inside her stilled. Waited. Anticipation hung in the air and a heaviness centered in the middle of her chest. Apprehension, longing, the pressure of indecision.

And then the tension snapped.

Jameson's mouth found hers. One hand buried in her hair as the other found purchase around her hip.

He clung to her, urging her to open and take. To give him everything that she'd been holding back.

Overwhelmed by the sensations he created, every instinct begged her to run. Like always. But there was nowhere to go. And she really didn't want to walk away from him—from this—anyway. That was fear of the unexpected and unknown talking and she was so tired of running.

His hands found the tie at her back and tugged the bow open. The second knot behind her neck followed as the top to her bikini fluttered to their feet.

Her own hands raced across his skin, chest, shoulders, hips. The rough texture of hair scraped against her palms, sending tingling sensations straight up her arms.

Kinley found the tie to his trunks and tugged the knot free. Material slithered down his hips with a hiss to settle on the floor beneath him. Without breaking the connection of their kiss, Jameson stepped free and kicked them away.

Her own bottoms joined the litter of clothing until they were both stark naked, nothing except the waning rays of sunshine painting their skin.

Wrapping an arm around her waist, Jameson boosted her up. Kinley didn't hesitate to wrap her legs tight around his body. The long ridge of his erection nestled between them, rubbing deliciously against the slippery entrance to her sex.

Kinley writhed in his arms, desperately trying to take every piece of him that she could. Mouth, fingers, arms and chest, every connection bombarded her senses.

She knew he moved because the world spun around her. Or maybe that was just her own equilibrium taking a hit. Her spine collided with something solid. Cool against her heated skin, she didn't even care what it was.

Jameson used the leverage to let go, sliding one hand along the center of her body. His gaze followed, devouring every inch of her skin. His fingers stopped to tug and tease.

"You're going to be the death of me," he grumbled, even as he leaned forward to tug a taut nipple deep into his mouth. The suction had Kinley's hips surging forward and her head dropping backward. A guttural sound echoed through her chest.

She had no idea where the condom came from, but it really didn't matter. The rustle caught her attention enough so that she watched him open the packet and roll the disc of latex down his erection.

Kinley's mouth went dry with anticipation as Jameson positioned his cock at the entrance to her body. With one fluid motion, he slid home deep inside.

Another sound, ecstasy and relief, fell from her parted lips. His strong arms held her up as his head dipped into the crook of her shoulder. His warm breath panted against her skin.

"Move, God, please," she begged when all he did was stand still, holding them both tight together. She tried to grind against him, to find relief from the ache, but his body pinned her against the wall.

"Shhh, slow," he whispered, right before his hips started moving.

Everything inside her screamed for fast. For the balm only he could give her. But that wasn't what he had in mind. His long, slow, steady strokes drove her insane. His mouth and hands only added to the mix, worshipping the rest of her body even as he built the pressure deep inside her higher and higher.

Kinley strained for release, practically begging with each panting breath.

"Trust me," he whispered. "Let go."

And Kinley was powerless to do anything else. The orgasm slammed into her with a force that grayed out the world around her, made everything except Jameson disappear. Her body pulsed around his, and if it wasn't for his strong arms holding her up, she would have slumped to the ground.

But Jameson wasn't ready to let her go. Her own body hummed and pulsed in the aftermath. But the tension quickly climbed again when he continued to thrust. Each long, hard stroke shot sparks through her body. And before long, she was groaning once again with the need for more.

This time, Kinley was aware enough to register Jameson's shuddering release. The way his body pulsed deep inside hers sent her own body hurtling over the edge again.

Together, they clung to each other, both propping

the other up. Her legs were shaky, so his had to be. After several moments, her breathing evened again and she started to squirm. Jameson backed away from the wall, but instead of letting her feet fall to the floor, he tightened his hold on her.

"Let me go," she murmured.

Bending over, he looked straight into her eyes and said, "Hell no." Her legs still wrapped around his waist, he headed for his stateroom. "We're nowhere close to finished."

Eleven

His fingers played lazily across her naked skin, drawing mindless patterns over her back and shoulder. A far cry from the last time they'd had sex, this time neither of them were playing games or in a hurry to leave.

"Your first hack?"

A smile teased her lips. "Just because I wanted to? There was a concert I wanted to attend, but I didn't have money for the tickets and my parents would never spend that kind of money on something I wanted."

He heard the bitterness in her voice. To anyone else, she might have sounded like a spoiled kid. Mom and Dad refused to buy an expensive ticket to a frivolous event. But after knowing her, Jameson recognized that it was more than that. It wasn't their refusal on this, it was their refusal on everything. Kinley's parents never saw her as anything more than a tool. A purpose. A means to an end. What she wanted never came into play.

"You hacked in and got tickets?"

Her smile widened and her bright blue eyes sparkled with the happy memory. "Front row."

"Who went with you?"

Kinley's eyebrows pulled in tight. "What do you mean? No one. I went by myself."

Jameson's chest ached and he had to consciously stop himself from rubbing against the pinch. A moment of teenage rebellion, and she hadn't had anyone to share it with. More than that, it hadn't occurred to her—even now—that she should have.

Folding her hands on his chest, Kinley let her chin drop as she watched him. "What about you?"

"Pretty typical and unimaginative. I was never very good in school."

"Bored?"

He answered with a hum of agreement. "I had a hard time concentrating on things that didn't seem to matter. Math and science I got. English, history, electives, foreign language…didn't care."

He remembered those days. The turmoil of his life playing out on so many fronts. "I was failing English. Had gotten into a huge fight with both my foster parents at the time. I knew I couldn't afford another bad grade so…"

"You changed your grade."

He shrugged. "Pretty boring."

The right corner of her lips curled up into a knowing grin. "That time. You didn't get caught."

No, he hadn't, although for the life of him he couldn't figure out how he'd avoided it. It wasn't like he'd been stealthy then. But it hadn't taken him long to become addicted to not only the adrenaline that came with taking a risk, but also the sense of power and accomplishment when he succeeded at solving the puzzle.

"How old were you?"

"Fourteen."

"Didn't take you long to go from run-of-the-mill to brilliant then, did it? Three years before an attempt at hacking into a government system."

Something kicked inside Jameson's chest. An old echo of the fear that never quite went away. The records surrounding that incident were sealed. For good reason. Only a handful of people were aware. But clearly, Kinley had gotten access.

"Apparently, not brilliant enough."

"Everyone slips up now and again."

"You?"

Her smile turned sardonic. "Even me."

"I shouldn't be surprised, but I am." He didn't even bother denying it; clearly there was no point.

Her soft laugh tickled against his skin. "No, you shouldn't be. I have to admit, I was surprised to discover that a man with a reputation for being mysterious, selective and careful with his clientele and reputation once worked for the government."

Perhaps she'd be surprised to hear that he still did.

Part of his reputation had been groundwork laid by his FBI and Homeland handlers. The money was entirely his, earned from legitimate corporate gigs and work with companies like Stone Surveillance. Good, legitimate hackers could set their own fees, especially when a company was in trouble.

"Part of my plea bargain was an agreement that I provide assistance whenever the government felt they needed it."

"You also did some time in a detention facility."

It wasn't a question. Jameson let his head drop against the headboard. Staring up at the ceiling, he let the tangled, twisted emotions wash over him. He'd learned, over the years, that it was best just to accept and breathe whenever the memories hit hard.

"Yeah, not that anyone cared. My parents were killed in a car accident when I was eleven. They were older when they had me, both single children. My grandparents died either before I was born or when I was very young. I had no one."

"And the government took advantage of that."

Jameson felt his shoulders shrug on pure muscle memory. He'd taught himself to shrug through the pain a long time ago.

"Maybe. I mean, there wasn't anyone to care or take me on. I'd been in foster care for years and was close to aging out of the system. In one sense, they did me a favor. Showed me a different path. Gave me a direction and purpose."

And in another, they took all sense of choice away from him.

When his parents died he had no one to comfort him. No one to help him deal with the devastation of losing the two people who meant the world to him. In one fell swoop he lost his parents, his life, the few friends he had and his home. His entire world turned upside down.

And just when he'd felt like he'd found someone who cared about him, that had come crashing down, too.

The memory of being alone and scared, unsure what to do, rushed through him. The feel of the stark plastic chair, so uncomfortable after being forced to sit there for hours and answer questions. Being overwhelmed as the attorney he'd been assigned and the agent in charge had explained the terms of his agreement with the government.

The overwhelming need for his parents. In reality, he'd still been a kid. That lost little boy. And in that moment he'd vowed to himself that he'd find a way back to the normal life and future he'd had with them. Before everything went wrong.

Kinley heard the devastation Jameson tried to hide. The vulnerability and loss behind the facade of strength and endurance. In that moment, she realized Jameson had grown up just as alone as she'd been.

Sure, she'd spent the last twelve years avoiding her parents, tracking them so that she could ensure they never crossed paths again, while his had been suddenly taken from him, but the result was that they'd both been left to fend for themselves.

The parallel was not lost on her. They'd both turned to hacking out of a necessity for survival, although the circumstances might have been slightly different. And even now, they were both products of their upbringing. Still alone.

Still lonely.

But, God, she didn't want to live her life that way anymore. Suddenly sad and weary, Kinley closed her eyes. A single unexpected tear dripped from the corner to fall with a silent plop onto Jameson's chest.

Grasping her, Jameson surged up, bringing them both to their knees. Leaning close, he wiped away the second tear that clung to her lashes. "Nope, no tears for me. I turned out just fine."

"Did you? Did either of us?" Her voice was low and rough, filled with gravel and regret. "We're not that different, are we? Our lives were turned upside down at a young age. We were forced to learn to rely on only ourselves. And we're still living those lessons. Mistrust, solitude, distance."

Kinley hadn't realized just how true her words were until they were out of her mouth. They'd spent the last several days at odds with each other, both at cross-purposes even if their goal was the same. Maybe if they'd worked together from the beginning, they'd have something to show for the days that had passed. Instead, her money was still gone, someone had threatened her, and they were stuck in the middle of the ocean.

Although maybe that worked in her favor since

whoever had left her that note probably couldn't track her here.

"I don't trust you, and you don't trust me, but we really have no reason for that, other than a history that has nothing to do with each other." Okay, strictly speaking, that might not be entirely true since Jameson *had* stolen her money. But she honestly did believe that his purpose had been genuine, even if his methods sucked.

Or maybe she just wanted to think that. Either way, what more did she have to lose?

"You asked me before who I thought might be after me."

"And you didn't really answer."

No, she had, but just not all of the answer. "I mean, I've pissed off lots of powerful people and they all might have an axe to grind. But I didn't share anything about my last job…or the one I'm currently working."

Which happened to be connected.

Kinley swiped Jameson's shirt off the floor. Tugging it over her head—she felt like she needed a little bit of armor before ripping herself entirely open—she crossed her legs at the end of the bed. Following her lead, Jameson tugged the covers up over his lap and settled against the headboard.

She wanted to point out that while he'd taken away some of the distraction, his naked, ripped and mesmerizing chest was still on display. Forcing her gaze away, she wrinkled her nose as she looked into his expectant eyes.

The warning bells in her head kept screaming at her to stop. But for once she ignored them. And maybe she'd regret that later, but right now, she didn't.

"Normally, the jobs I pull are in and out. Steal the money, distribute it to people who need it."

"Restore balance to the universe."

A tangled sound, half laugh and half groan, fell from her lips. "I'm no superhero."

"Could have fooled me."

Did he really see her that way? Part of her wanted to ask the question, but the rest of her didn't want to know the answer. In case he was just playing with her or giving her a hard time.

"Anyway, this job was different."

"Different how?"

"The more I dug…the worse it got. I've dealt with some pretty nasty people over the years. I've targeted arms dealers. Cartel. Mobsters on multiple continents. Generally, the scum of society. People who prey on the weak, the innocent."

"Those who can't defend themselves." Jameson's pointed tone wasn't lost on her. No, it didn't take a psych degree to figure out she spent her life's work trying to right the wrongs she was unwittingly involved in committing during those years with her parents.

Know better, do better and all that.

"Sure. That's some of it anyway. I even uncovered a trafficking ring in the Balkans several years ago."

Jameson's brow wrinkled. "What you uncovered this time was worse than selling people?"

Even now, just speaking about it had her stomach tied in knots. Not because the crimes were heinous, although they were, but because she was powerless to do anything about it.

"Worse in the sense of an utter abuse of power. Most of the people I target don't work too hard to hide exactly what they are. These people…pure treachery masquerading as good."

And maybe that was what made her so sick. The realization that so many had no idea what the people they trusted to look out for their best interests were capable of.

"It started as an opportunity to drain some corrupt politicians in Europe of capital. Take their money, thwart their influence. But the more threads I pulled, the more tangled I realized the web went. I wasn't just dealing with a few rotten apples, I was dealing with a network of connected allies who hardly had the interests of their countries at heart. Not only that, but the network they operate under is a well-known international charitable organization."

"Would I know it?"

"Probably. One Peace."

Jameson's reaction had been hers as well. The utter shock followed by disbelief and then overwhelming anger. One Peace was the international charity that ran commercials highlighting the disasters and humanitarian efforts they were involved with around the world.

Earthquakes, civil unrest, terrorism and human

rights violations. They provided assistance and funding for good works in almost every country.

Every civilized country contributed in an effort to pool resources for the highest good. Hell, the board of directors comprised some of the biggest political and business names in the world, not just the US.

Or that's what she'd thought. Until she'd begun investigating the corrupt politicians and discovered their ties to the organization. At first, she'd assumed the connection had been one of convenience. Their political standing offered them access.

But the more she'd dug, the more threads had unraveled, until she'd realized everyone involved at the top of the organization had their fingers in the corruption.

They used the guise of the charity to gain access to highly classified information and use it for their own gain. They manipulated markets, inflated the cost of medical supplies, sold arms and in several instances had directly manipulated situations to cause the event they then swooped in to "save" people from.

"You're kidding."

Kinley let out a humorless laugh. "I wish."

"How high up? How far does this reach?"

"You know the organization. Almost every developed country has high-level representatives. The US, France, Spain, Japan, England, Sweden, Denmark…" Her voice tailed off.

"I get the picture."

"I took as much funding as I could get my hands on from the politicians who were my original target, but the problem is there's plenty more and that hardly made a dent in the resources One Peace has."

Lifting the necklace she kept around her neck 24/7, Kinley held it between them. "I have hundreds, thousands of files with evidence right here on this flash drive. But I'm a hacker with no reputation."

Unlike Jameson, she'd worked hard to keep a low profile, not just in real life, but in her hacking life as well. She hadn't wanted the reputation. Never cared if people knew what she was doing. But now…that anonymity worked against her.

"I've been a ghost for the last twelve years. No one will listen to me or trust the information since it wasn't exactly obtained legally. Not to mention, I have no idea who to trust with it. When I say everyone is involved, I mean high-level government officials, media moguls, high-profile business executives. The kind of people who can make problems and stories go away."

Jameson simply stared at the flash drive disguised as jewelry for several seconds before finally switching his gaze to her.

"Motive for stealing from you?"

Kinley finally put words to the fear she hadn't wanted to admit. "Motive for a lot more, probably. I didn't mention it before because, well…"

"You didn't trust me." His words were grim, but true.

"I received an anonymous note right as I left to come to Tampa. Someone demanding money. It wasn't specific, so it could be from any of the people I've stolen from."

"But most likely it's from the politicians."

She shrugged. That's the conclusion she'd jumped to.

No, she hadn't wanted to be trapped on a yacht for the past few days—although sex with Jameson had been a nice bonus. But if she was honest, she'd been looking over her shoulder for weeks. And the note she'd received had really scared her. It had been nice to have a few days where she didn't feel hunted.

Although she wasn't ready to confess that to Jameson.

Reaching out, he ran his fingers through Kinley's hair. "Let me help."

Instinct had an argument jumping to her lips, but caution forced her to hold the words in. Wasn't she just spouting the idea that they both had difficulty trusting others and that if they'd worked together from the beginning, maybe they'd have gotten further than when they were working against each other?

Maybe it was time for her to take a leap of faith. "Okay."

Not for the first time, the contacts he'd cultivated both within the government and with Stone Surveillance paid off. It was interesting, walking both sides of a very distinct line. Both sides used him. Both sides benefited. And neither was entirely certain of how he obtained his knowledge, but they were both happy enough with the results that so far no one asked questions.

But it was tiresome, draining and lonely. Gray, and Stone had become the virtual port in the storm, true friends despite how their relationship had started. They were good men, which was why he felt guilty for what he and Kinley were about to do.

Because there was no doubt in his mind, Kinley was involved in something dangerous. Although that was hardly different from the status quo of her life for the past several years. He should ask for their help. He 100 percent knew they'd give it, no questions asked.

Well, Gray would ask several.

Kinley, though, wouldn't forgive him for betraying her trust. She'd finally confided in him and he couldn't use that against her. Not and hope to have anything when this was all finished.

If you'd asked him days ago if he'd wanted that or thought it was possible, Jameson would have laughed. But now...the idea that eventually Kinley would disappear back into her clandestine world made him sick.

He'd deal with that later, though. Right now, his gut was telling him if they found a way to bring down the people involved in the corruption ring she'd uncovered, they'd also follow the trail to her money.

It wasn't lost on him that the money provided her the means to leave. But it also was a barrier between them, one he needed to clear up before they could even think about anything further.

So Jameson had made a few phone calls, bargained a few favors and convinced an old acquaintance from the CIA—a contact he trusted implicitly—to meet with them in New Orleans.

Jameson had to admit to being slightly euphoric at the idea of being able to tell her they had a possible solution. Last night, when she'd finally trusted him enough to reveal what she'd been working on, he'd felt the weight of that. And understood her frustration and disappointment at having her hands tied.

Being the one to help her made him feel...powerful, useful, happy.

Walking out onto the sundeck, Jameson stopped and simply appreciated the view for several seconds. The swimsuit she'd picked today provided a little more coverage than the ones she'd been wearing. He wasn't sure whether to be disappointed or relieved. Either way, it wasn't like the extra fabric hid much.

Especially from his memory of her lithe body sliding against his. The feel of her skin beneath his fingers.

Shaking his head, Jameson forced himself to focus.

Today, she wore a large-brim straw hat. Her suit was white, which made her sun-bronzed skin pop, and one-piece, although strategic pieces of fabric had been cut out to leave spots of skin bare. Large glasses hid her eyes, so he couldn't be sure if she watched him.

Probably, although he'd gotten pretty good at feeling the weight of her gaze on him, even if he couldn't see her face.

Kinley Sullivan was gorgeous. But it wasn't just the perfect way her form and face came together. She was brilliant and tireless and had a huge heart, even if she tried to hide and protect it. Those were the things that made her intoxicatingly attractive.

"Why are you lurking there?"

Her voice startled him into action. Striding across

the deck, Jameson sat in the lounger beside her, but didn't bother lying back. Instead, he spread his knees wide and let his hands dangle between them.

He wasn't certain how she'd react.

"I spoke with my contact and she's agreed to meet us in New Orleans tonight."

Kinley tipped the glasses down her nose so she could peer over them. "Tonight, huh?" A single eyebrow quirked up in question. And, almost as if the universe had planned it, the engines kicked on and the *Queen* began to slowly move forward. "So much for mechanical failure."

He looked faintly embarrassed as he shrugged. "Blame me, not Eric."

"Oh, there's plenty of blame to go around. But I am curious as to what he was doing banging about in the engine room the other night."

It was his turn to raise an eyebrow. "You mean the night you sneaked out of my bed to snoop around the ship?"

Her mouth twisted and to his surprise a blush stained her cheeks. "I won't apologize for that."

"Never expected you would."

Leaning closer, he leveled his gaze straight at hers. "I don't like being used."

She shot back immediately, "I don't like being trapped."

"Fair enough."

Shifting, Kinley moved farther into his space. "But just so we're clear, what happened between us that night…it wasn't my intention. My plan was just to flirt, tease, maybe get you drunk. Once I started, I couldn't stop."

The confession shot through him, burning into his belly and leaking fire into his blood like the strongest whiskey. God, he wanted her. "Thank you."

"For what?"

"Telling me the truth."

With a sigh, she sagged against her chair. "No reason to lie. Last night pretty much proved neither of us are good at keeping our hands to ourselves."

Her tone of voice made it sound like they were afflicted with some fatal illness. "There are worse things in the world, Kinley."

Grabbing a handful of his shirt, she jerked him down and claimed his mouth. "True," she murmured.

Jameson let the need for her crash over him. They had several hours to kill before docking in New Orleans anyway. Plenty of time to worry and deal with the inevitable.

Logically he realized heading to dry land was the right thing to do. They couldn't sit out here in the middle of the Gulf indefinitely.

But, God, he hoped he wasn't making a mistake trusting her. There was no doubt in his mind that Kinley had the ability to simply slip away.

Now was the time to trust that she wouldn't.

Twelve

She should be pissed. Considering how quickly the Queen had begun to move, clearly there'd been nothing wrong with her. Jameson had lied to her.

But then, she'd lied to him.

Two wrongs didn't make a right, but in this case maybe they just canceled each other out. She did have a habit of running. And if they'd headed to New Orleans a few days ago, that's most likely what she would have done.

It irked her that Jameson knew her well enough to recognize that little fact when she hadn't even been conscious of it herself. Her entire life she'd been running…had it simply become habit?

For the first time since connecting all the dots on One Peace, and realizing she had no one to turn to with the information, Kinley began to feel optimistic. Maybe, just maybe, things were going to work out. These people would be brought to justice and she could get her life back.

Not to mention her money.

Although even without the safety net of the money, the pit in the middle of her belly had slowly disappeared. For the first time in her life, Kinley had a sense of...optimism. Everything would be okay.

It was early evening when they pulled into the marina. Standing on the sundeck, she'd watched the city come into focus, bright lights, tall buildings and the evidence of civilization spread wide before her.

"I've never been to New Orleans." Somehow the statement felt like a confession, even if it wasn't. For the past several years she'd rarely set foot back in the US. At first, she'd been afraid of her father and mother's reach. Then it didn't feel like home.

She felt the weight of Jameson's gaze and heard the smile in his voice when he said, "Maybe we'll have time for a little sightseeing, but first, we're heading to the meet with my contact. At a masquerade."

Excitement and the sharp edge of anticipation pulsed beneath Kinley's skin. It took them so long to dock and disembark from the ship. Jameson grasped her hand as they walked through the marina to a large Jeep waiting for them. He settled her into the passenger seat before walking around to get behind the wheel.

Wind whipped through her hair, sending it dancing around her face, but she didn't care. Glancing at her, laughter in those gorgeous green eyes, Jameson reached into the console and handed her a hair band.

The exhilaration only increased when they reached the hustle and bustle of the French Quarter. Pulling up to one of the boutique hotels, Jameson tossed the keys to the valet and grabbed both bags. She hadn't even realized they'd been packed or back there.

Less than an hour after pulling into the city, they were ensconced in a luxurious hotel room and entirely alone for the first time in days.

As soon as the door closed behind them, Kinley shot across the room, grasped a handful of his shirt and pulled him in for a soul-stirring kiss. Heat and need flamed bright between them, overwhelming and all-consuming. It blocked out everything except the two of them.

Kinley fumbled with the button on her shorts but gave up when it wouldn't cooperate. Instead, she concentrated on getting him naked, reaching for his shirt and pulling it over his head.

Jameson's hands clamped on her wrists, stalling her movements.

"As much as I want this—" the smoldering heat in his expression left no doubt he meant the words "—we don't have time."

An unhappy groan rumbled through her chest. "Are you sure?"

"We're meeting my contact in exactly one hour."

Kinley let out a huge sigh. "Fine." Turning to the bags he'd dropped inside the door, she discovered the first was packed with his things. The second revealed stuff for her. Snatching it up, she marched into the bathroom. "If I can't have you, I'll take a hot shower."

Snapping the door closed between them, she couldn't stop her own grin at the sound of his laughter.

It didn't take her long to get ready. As always, the crew from the ship knew exactly what she'd needed and she'd nearly gasped when she'd pulled out the dress, shoes and matching mask.

Deep red velvet, the neckline curved in the shape of a heart right above her breasts. It cinched in at the waist before belling out in a wide skirt that fell just below her knees. Simple and elegant, the dress made her feel utterly decadent.

It was quintessential New Orleans.

The shoes were perfection. Tiny black straps crisscrossed up her feet, ankles and calves. Attached to not much more than a sole and a four-inch heel, they gave her height that she didn't really need.

A light hand with makeup and a quick touch with a curling wand had a cascade of curls rioting down her shoulders. A sultry reflection stared back.

The mask sitting silently on the vanity would complete the outfit. Dramatic black lace and feathers. The large plume on one side worked perfectly to obscure half her face. The scrolling black edge of lace around her eyes, cheeks and nose did the rest.

Hopefully, no one could recognize her.

The minute she stepped out of the bathroom Jameson's mouth dropped open.

"Jesus, woman, we're supposed to blend in," he growled.

Kinley looked at herself, puzzled, before glancing up. "What's wrong with my dress?"

"Nothing. Everything."

Jameson strode across the room. He wasn't soft as he grabbed her, pulled her against his body and kissed the hell out of her. The scent of him, intoxicating and inviting, teased at her senses. She melted against him, letting her body relax and give even as her mouth demanded more from him.

Always, she wanted more.

Breaking the kiss, Jameson took a step back. His gaze prowled over her. "The Queen of Hearts," he breathed, reverence and appreciation filling the words.

He shoved his hands into the pocket of his black tux.

Her body hummed, echoes of the soft caress of his hands along her skin.

"You look amazing."

Kinley gave him a lopsided smile. "That's what happens when you put a girl in expensive shoes."

His mouth found hers again, words whispered against her lips before he claimed them as his own. "The shoes have nothing to do with it."

Happiness bubbled in her belly, an unexpected sensation.

"We need to get out of this room right now, or we won't be leaving it for the next three days."

Another burst of heat broke over her. Grasping her hand, Jameson led them through the hotel. A set of double glass doors whooshed open, letting in the oppressive heat and the noise from the street.

It wasn't Mardi Gras, but New Orleans still knew how to have a good time and host a mean party.

Lights, sounds, laughter and color bombarded her. Jameson kept a firm hold of her hand as they entered the flow of people moving through the street. He used his body to create an opening they could both move through. Bodies weaved in and out. Music rose and fell as they passed bars and restaurants packed with people.

Leaning forward, she asked, "Where are we going?"

"The far end of the street to a small, private club."

She wanted to ask him why they'd stayed so far away but decided it didn't matter. She was enjoying the experience and maybe when they were done they'd have the chance to participate in the fun, not just walk through it.

They were moving quickly when Jameson veered across the flow of people toward the opposite side of the road. Kinley stumbled on a piece of uneven sidewalk, the movement jostling her hand from his.

Someone pushed against her, sending her off-balance in the opposite direction. An arm wrapped around her shoulders, taking her weight and guiding her through the melee toward an opening between buildings. At first, Kinley assumed it was Jameson, until a dark voice whispered in her ear.

"Can't be too careful."

The menacing tone had Kinley jerking her head up. Unsteady, she felt like the world was whirling around her when she found Jameson several feet away, staring at her. His mouth opened, as if he were yelling, but she couldn't hear the words over the noise.

The arm around her shoulder tightened and another around her waist joined in, jerking her off her feet entirely. In that moment, she realized she was standing at the opening of a dark alley, and someone was pulling her inside.

Jameson had never been so scared in his life. Watching from several feet away, the swirling crush of people separating them, as Kinley was yanked off her feet and pulled into a small opening between buildings. Her skirt flared; her feet kicked.

And then she was just…gone.

Pushing against the crowd, he yelled for everyone to get out of his way. Someone shoved back, but he didn't care. He had to get to her before she disappeared.

His heart raced painfully inside his chest. He was only a few moments behind, but he half expected to see the alley empty. So he was relieved at the outline of two shadowy figures on the far end. Walls, dark with age and grime, rose high on either side. They blocked the noise of the street, muting the party they'd left behind.

"Let go of me!" The strong sound of Kinley's voice had relief flooding through his system.

No, not yet. She wasn't safe yet.

Kinley kicked, using the heel of her shoes to connect with anything she could find. The man holding her grunted. Score one for Kinley. She squirmed, her arms and legs flailing against her assailant. Thank God her struggles were slowing them.

The man—Jameson assumed it was a man based on stature alone—was dressed in black from head to toe. He wore a surgical mask over his nose and mouth and the hood from his sweatshirt was up, obscuring almost every distinguishing feature. With the long shadows and encroaching night, Jameson couldn't tell much of anything.

The man could be twenty or sixty. Any race or nationality. One thing was clear, he was huge. And so far, appeared to be working alone.

Jameson didn't hesitate. The moment he reached them he entered the fray. Rearing back, he let his fist fly and connected with something solid. The man grunted. His head snapped. But he didn't let Kinley go.

One second she was fighting and yelling, the next she went limp in her assailant's arms. Another spurt of fear shot through his system. Had the man knocked her out?

No, he couldn't let that distract him. He needed to get her away and safe and then they could deal with any potential injuries.

The man, apparently deciding that with Kinley limp, Jameson was the bigger threat, dropped the arm around her shoulders and used it to pull a knife from somewhere.

Damn.

What little light there was hit the blade, glinting through the gloomy shadows and showing off the deadly serrated edge. Jameson's entire being was focused on that knife.

"Back off," the man commanded in a low, menacing voice.

"Okay." Jameson held up his hands in the universal symbol for surrender. But there was no way he'd leave Kinley alone and vulnerable. Not while he was still standing.

Taking a single step back, he feinted to the side and then launched himself forward, all the while focusing on that knife.

He'd learned a thing or two in his life, and not just the skills acquired sitting in front of his computer. Driving the palm of his hand into the shoulder of the arm holding the knife, his intention was to startle the man and stun his arm. Both apparently worked because his fingers opened, and the blade clattered to the ground.

In that same moment, Kinley surged upward. With only a single arm around her waist, and her assailant's distraction, she managed to untangle herself. She tumbled to the ground but was already scrambling on hands and knees to get up.

The minute she found her feet and surged away, Jameson followed. At first, he ran backward to keep the stranger in his sights. But when he made no move to follow, Jameson turned and sprinted.

The lights and noise of the Quarter swirled around them as they burst through to the sidewalk. Jameson collided with someone and offered an automatic apology even as his gaze scoured the people in front of him.

Where was she?

A few feet away, Kinley sagged against an older gentleman. Clearly a tourist, he was holding her up even as his gaze searched the people around him looking for help. "Are you okay, ma'am?"

Jameson reached them and snatched her up into his own arms. Pulling the phone from his pocket, he called Eric. "We're in the Quarter. Have the car meet us. Now." He didn't even wait for a response before hanging up. He had no doubt Eric would track his exact location through his phone.

Crouching so that he could look her in the eye, he expected to see tears or fear or shock or all three in Kinley's gaze. So he was startled to see pure unadulterated fire instead.

But he probably shouldn't have been. Kinley wasn't hurt, she was pissed.

"Are you okay?" He asked the question anyway, mostly because he needed to hear the answer. The older man she'd collided with hovered above them, waiting for her answer as well.

"No, I'm not okay."

Not what he was looking for.

And apparently not what the man loitering wanted to hear either. The other man pushed his way into the conversation. "Ma'am, is this man bothering you? Do you need help?"

Kinley glanced up, shaking her head. "No. It's fine. He's fine."

Jameson looked around them, realizing they'd drawn a small crowd. Both good and bad. At least anyone watching them would think twice about making another attempt to grab Kinley while they were the focus of so much attention.

Kinley apparently didn't care who was watching or listening.

"I have no idea who that was. He snatched me right off the street in the middle of a crowd."

"Yes, I know. I was there." And he didn't think he'd ever forget those moments of helplessness and undiluted fear.

To his surprise, Kinley shook out of his hold, pushed up off the curb and headed to the alley. Following, he snagged her elbow and stopped her. "What the hell do you think you're doing?"

Her hair was disheveled, a tangled mass of rioting dark waves in her face. Her dress was ruined, covered in grime he didn't even want to name. There was a smudge of dirt across one cheek and the beginnings of a bruise near her temple.

She'd never looked so amazing to him. Because the anger in her eyes and the color in her cheeks said she was alive and safe.

"To find out who that was and what they want."

"No."

"What do you mean, no?"

His phone vibrated. Jameson didn't bother looking at it. He knew it was a text telling him the car was close.

"First, the man is long gone. He didn't strike me as the type to loiter at the scene of a crime."

A frustrated growl rolled up Kinley's throat.

"Second, he isn't going to tell you anything, but

might try—and succeed this time—to take you. Only a fool confronts an enemy without the advantage and a plan."

Her mouth twisted, but she stopped pulling against his hold. "What are you, some strategy expert now?"

"Yes, we both are. We employ strategy every day, Kinley. You're pissed. So am I."

"Could have fooled me."

"But we gain nothing right now by staying here. We need to get to the yacht where I can guarantee your safety and we can figure out what the hell just happened."

"I know what just happened. An asshole tried to kidnap me off the street."

She'd nailed it in one, although her assessment was a simplistic view of the events. He wanted to know who and why. Needed to know so he could keep her safe.

Needed to analyze this clear increase in the danger she was in…and call on reinforcements.

He'd never forget the helpless sensation of watching her just…disappear. And realizing that he'd never forgive himself if something happened to her because he was being stupid and not using every resource at their disposal. She didn't want to deal with her brother or her past right now. He got it. But that was just too bad.

Although she wasn't in a frame of mind to listen or agree with him, so that was a confrontation for another time. Right now, he needed to get her off the street.

This time, she didn't protest as he wrapped an arm around her waist and headed away from Bourbon Street. His shoulders tightened and his neck tingled as they left the noise and people behind. But hyper-aware of his surroundings, Jameson was certain they weren't followed. This time.

The Jeep wasn't far. Boosting her up into it, he didn't bother taking the wheel from Eric, who sat in the driver's seat. "Get us out of here. Fast."

His captain simply nodded. The force of their speed pushed them against the seats. Buying the Wrangler with the V-8 Hemi was paying off. Jameson had no idea how long it took them to get back to the marina. Longer than he would have liked. He kept hold of Kinley's hand the entire way, needing that tangible connection to her to steady his own nerves.

She was fine. Whole and safe.

By the time they arrived at the *Queen*, his heart had finally slowed. Kinley slammed the door open and jumped from the truck. She stomped up the gang-way and onto the ship. Clearly, while the drive had settled him it had served to stoke her anger higher.

He followed, a little slower, as she entered the salon. Pausing at the bar, she unscrewed the cap on a bottle of tequila, poured two shots and downed one with barely a pause. She held the other out to him, and Jameson took it and swallowed the liquor. It burned down his throat and into his gut.

Dropping the glass onto the sideboard, he pushed

into her personal space. Grasping her chin, he tilted her head for a better look at the bruise.

"I'm fine." Her words were hard as nails.

Sweeping his thumb over the tight pink bow of her mouth, he said, "What you are, is amazing."

Thirteen

She didn't feel amazing. What she felt was shaky and pissed and fearful. And she was working over-time not to show any of it. Because if she fell apart now, she wasn't certain she'd be able to find all the pieces and fit them together again.

Better to focus on moving forward rather than what might have happened if that man had succeeded in getting her out of that alley.

"Why are we at the yacht and not the hotel?"

Better to focus on facts and truths, figuring out how to escape from this mess with her life. Because it was clear someone wanted to seriously hurt her.

"Because my assumption is we were followed from the hotel, so it isn't safe."

"But the yacht is?"

Jameson's lips turned into a tight frown. "Not necessarily, but my staff is excellent, and they've been following standard security protocol since we docked. I can guarantee no one's been close to the *Queen*. At the moment, we're safer here than anywhere else."

The relief that rushed through her almost sent her to her knees. It was pure and unexpected and packed a punch. Grasping the edge of the sideboard, Kinley fought to keep herself upright and steady.

But something must have given her away.

Cupping her by the elbow, Jameson guided her to one of the overstuffed chairs. He swiveled it out as he pressed her into the plush cushions.

Kinley wasn't used to being taken care of. Even as a child, she never had a classic mother or father who cared. No one kissed her boo-boos or told her there were no monsters under the bed. When she hurt herself, the best she got was a "suck it up, buttercup" and a tube of antibiotic ointment tossed in her general direction. Even as a toddler, she'd learned to take care of herself.

So it was unsettling to have someone else trying to fill that role. But even as much as she didn't want it to be, it was also pleasant. This was the second time he'd taken care of her in a crisis, and as she blinked up at him, Kinley realized she could get used to having him take care of her.

Which scared her and made her yearn for something she hadn't even realized she'd wanted.

Crouching in front of her, Jameson braced his hands on the arms of the chair. The scent of him teased her nose and forced her mind onto something other than the experience she'd left behind.

"What next?" The question felt foreign in her mouth. Racking her brain, Kinley tried to think of a time in her life she'd ever asked someone that question. She was the one who formed plans and executed them. Alone. But right now, her brain was off-kilter and she didn't trust her own analytical skills.

Surprisingly enough, she did trust him, though.

"Clearly, One Peace isn't going to stop at simply getting their money back. They must know the information you have and want it and you."

What kind of hell had she gotten herself into? "I didn't ask for this." This job had started like any other, an attempt to drain funds from a few corrupt people. But it had ballooned into something bigger than she could handle.

Bigger than they could handle?

Jameson opened his mouth to respond, but Eric entered the room, distracting him. "You have a call on the sat phone."

Surging to his feet, Jameson frowned even as he glanced at her. "I'll be right back."

Kinley wanted to protest. Or follow him. But she wouldn't let herself be that kind of woman. Clearly, whoever was calling him had urgent business or they wouldn't have contacted the ship. They also knew how to find him, so it had to be someone close. Maybe a client?

Rachel appeared in front of her, holding out a glass. Kinley half expected it to be something strong, but on the first sip realized the other woman had handed her ice water.

Until that moment, she hadn't realized just how dry her throat was. In fact, she'd devoured almost the entire glass by the time Jameson returned to the salon.

His lips were a thin, tight line as he issued an order to Eric. "Prepare to sail as soon as possible."

"No." The word was out of Kinley's mouth before she'd even realized she was saying it. "I'm so tired of running, Jameson."

His pale green eyes narrowed. "This isn't running. This is regrouping."

Shaking her head, Kinley stepped into his space. The heat of him touched her, melting across her skin. She could have reached for him. Wanted the reassurance of his solid form beneath her fingertips.

But she didn't.

Because she needed a clear mind to articulate her point, and because she didn't want to use their physical connection to cloud his judgment. She needed him to understand her position and support her because he believed in her.

"Sure it is. And I would know. I've been running for years." Suddenly, a wave of exhaustion washed over her, pressing against every fiber of her being and threatening to drown her.

"That life might be one I chose. And helping people, taking care of those who can't help themselves, has been worth the sacrifice. But I'm tired. Of being alone. Of constantly looking over my shoulder. Wondering when that unexpected bullet is going to hit. Never trusting anyone."

She rested her hand on his arm and forced herself not to close her eyes at the rush of awareness and need that stormed through her system.

"I need to end this. Now. If I don't, I'm afraid it'll never stop."

Slowly, Jameson's fingers brushed against the bruise at the edge of her hairline. His expression went soft, almost apologetic. Kinley's shoulders sagged, certain that he wouldn't listen to her plea.

"I promise, we're not giving up."

She'd be pissed at him, but Jameson could think of no other way to keep her safe. Watching her get pulled into that alley...those were the worst moments of his life. When he'd thought she was gone.

And he would do absolutely anything to make sure that didn't happen.

So he was calling in the one person he knew had the contacts and resources to help them. The one person she'd already said plainly she wasn't ready to see.

He could have warned her. Maybe he should have. But there was a part of him afraid that even though they'd pulled into open waters—admittedly not very far from shore—she'd find a way off the ship.

So instead, he put off the inevitable. It would be morning before Gray joined them on board anyway. In the meantime, he'd take the opportunity to reassure himself they were both alive.

Sweeping her into his arms, Jameson carried her

into his cabin. Setting her onto her feet, he carefully peeled the ruined dress from her body. Kneeling before her, his fingers wrapped around her ankle as he removed each of the delicate shoes from her feet.

Running warm water in the shower, he gently guided her inside and washed every inch of her body, taking the time to catalog and evaluate every bruise, scratch and scrape on her skin. She didn't have anything that would require more than antibiotic ointment and time to heal.

Loving her was slow. Heat built between them, a gentle swell that crested over them both, sweeping them deeper under the connection they shared.

Neither of them said anything, but then they didn't have to. When they were both exhausted and replete, Jameson toweled them off and gently placed Kinley in the center of his bed. He wrapped his arms around her and was gratified that she drifted off almost immediately.

Because she felt safe in his arms? That was a question he wasn't ready to ask her. Because he knew the answer he wanted and wasn't certain he'd get it.

Jameson lay there for a long time, unable to close his own eyes because each time he did the scene in that alley played out again. Over and over, with varying endings, none of them good.

Kinley shifted. The necklace she always wore brushed against the back of his hand. He looked at the twisted hunk of metal. And he realized the problem in all of this wasn't the money. It was the data on that tiny drive. That information was what was putting her in danger.

He stared at the half that was still there, assuming the actual drive had fallen out during the attempt to take her. Clearly, Kinley hadn't recognized that it was missing. Part of him wished the disappearance would mean her safety, but there was no way to prove to anyone that the information was gone.

Kinley would be devastated.

Until she realized he'd taken the drive and copied it…while she was asleep.

A single beam of sunlight slashed across her face. Squinting, Kinley opened her eyes and nearly let out an audible groan. Her brain felt fuzzy and a dull headache pounded right behind her eyes. Her whole body felt tight, every muscle unhappy.

Forcing herself to sit up, she rubbed the heels of her palms into her eyes and took several deep, even breaths. Walking into the bathroom, she splashed cold water on her face and felt a little better.

She didn't have time to wallow. No, Jameson had distracted her last night and she still needed to convince him to head back to New Orleans so they could finish this once and for all.

Grabbing the clothes that were set out on the bench on the far wall, she tried not to think about who on staff had gotten the shorts, bra, T-shirt and panties from her room and laid them out for her.

Nope, not embarrassing at all.

Armor on, she headed up to the deck. She could

see the top of Jameson's head over a chair. What gave her pause was the second head and the murmur of two male voices. In all the days they'd been on the *Queen*, never once had she seen any of the staff sitting. Oh, she had no doubt they did, just not where she'd seen them.

So who was Jameson talking to? Maybe his FBI contact?

Striding across the deck, Kinley approached on Jameson's right. Leaning over, she placed a kiss to his lips and murmured, "I missed waking up beside you," before straightening to take in the other man.

And froze solid.

Fight-or-flight instinct flooded her body, kicking her heart into overdrive and sending a cascade of dread into her belly. If Jameson weren't holding tightly to her hand, she might have turned and fled.

Shock, fear, hope and devastation all tangled inside as she stared into her brother's deep eyes.

"Good morning." His voice was modulated and careful, even on the two innocuous words.

She had no idea what to say. No idea what she wanted.

No, that wasn't true. If she was honest, she'd played this moment out in her head so many times. Each of the scenarios had begun with her brother yelling at her.

So far, not only wasn't he yelling, but he appeared to be waiting for her.

"Gray." The single word wheezed out of her tight chest.

Reaching behind her, Jameson dragged another

chair across the deck and gently pushed her into it. "Breathe, Kinley. I promise he's here to help."

Her gaze jerked to Jameson's for the first time since she'd recognized her brother. "You're not surprised. You knew he was coming." Her brain kept racing. "He was the call last night. You knew last night?"

Jameson reached for her again, but this time she didn't let him touch her. Instead, she shoved his hand away. "No." Rising from the chair, she challenged him. "You should have told me."

"Why? What would you have done?" Jameson's cool, calm demeanor as he gazed up at her set her teeth on edge. Her belly was roiling with a boa constrictor–sized knot of emotions. And he was a convenient target for the worst of them.

"I don't know. Something."

"Like jump overboard? We both know you run, Kinley. But Gray can help. He wants to help."

Kinley's gaze leaped across to her brother's again. Head tilted, he simply watched the exchange, neither confirming nor denying Jameson's statement.

Jameson slowly rose, breaking the contact of Gray's gaze. Shifting, he went to step around her. When she realized he intended to leave, instinct had her hand shooting out to stop him.

Kinley might be mad at him—oh, was she ever—but she also didn't want him to go. Because that would leave her alone with her brother, and she was nowhere ready for that.

Jameson stepped closer into her personal space,

and she tried not to let out a sigh of relief. Really, she was stronger than this, wasn't she?

Looking up into his gaze, she could see the reflection of her own fear staring at her in Jameson's eyes. Leaning forward, he brushed his mouth across hers and whispered, "Trust me," before untangling her fingers from his arm and walking away.

Inside her chest, Kinley's heart raced. But her gaze was inexorably drawn to the man waiting several feet away. Gray silently watched her out of dark, deep eyes. There was no judgment. No disdain or anger. Simply a deep well of understanding. Acceptance.

The lump in her throat swelled, a pressure so hard to ignore.

Slowly, Gray pushed up and out of his chair. He crossed the deck to her, inches away. The child in her- the one who had wished for a sibling, to not be alone- wanted nothing more than to lean into him, hug him, but she couldn't let herself make that first move. Comfort was something she didn't deserve and had no right to take from him.

But Gray offered it to her anyway. Wrapping an arm around her shoulders, he pulled her tight into the shelter of his body. And somehow Kinley found herself, face buried in his warm chest, letting it all go. Tears flowed, not just the ones she'd been holding back for the past several days, but the ones she hadn't let herself shed for years.

Gray said nothing. He didn't offer empty words that couldn't heal the wounds. He didn't promise her everything would be okay. He simply held her. And when the tears stopped and her chest felt light and empty for the first time in as long as she could remember, he eased back to look at her.

"I'm sorry."

If she'd had any tears left, she might have shed a few more. "You're apologizing? For what? I ruined your life, Gray. You'll never know how sorry I am for that."

His stark mouth twisted into a grin, something instinct told her didn't happen very often. "Oh, I know. Your actions scream plenty loud enough that you're sorry. You've spent years making yourself a target by trying to atone for what you unwittingly did. You were a pawn, Kinley, and I know that. You don't have a mean bone in your body."

She huffed. "Maybe you don't know me."

He rolled his eyes and play-punched her shoulder. "Maybe not, but I really want to."

"Why didn't you come after me?"

Gray leaned against the railing and stared up into the bright morning sky. "From what little I know you've been manipulated your entire life. I didn't want to be one more person who disregarded what you wanted or needed. Coming to me, wanting to be a part of my life, had to be your choice. So I gave you space to make it."

"What if I never did?"

The smirk on his face and the twinkle in his eyes were contagious and she felt the kernel of an answering euphoria deep in her belly. "Oh, I was almost to the point of giving you a few nudges. Blakely- we're married now and she is dying to see you again,- jokes about my patience, but there is a limit."

"Oh, so making up my own mind only goes so far, huh? You're as bad as Jameson."

His grin widened. "Worse. I'm looking forward to figuring out how to be a big brother and I have some years of being a pain in your backside to catch up on."

Okay, this would be way better than anything she could have imagined.

And then the humor in his eyes died, crashing her down to reality. "Trust me, Joker told me what's happening and everyone at Stone Surveillance is ready to help. We'll find a way out of this mess for you. That's our job and we're very good at it. I have no doubt Stone is already working on a strategy back in Charleston.

"We'll figure out what happens after that. But no matter what, I want you in my life, Kinley. You and I get to decide what that looks like. Our mom is a piece of work and our dads aren't much better. We both grew up with shitty parents and have been knocked around by circumstances. But we turned out pretty okay. You're family, the only one I have left. And I really don't want to lose the opportunity to build a relationship with you. If you'll let me."

Okay, she was wrong. There were more tears because the backs of her eyes stung with them. Fear and years of self-preservation were difficult to counter, but she wanted to. "I want that, too. I'm so tired of being alone, Gray. I was so worried you would hate me. Blame me. And I wouldn't have faulted you."

"I don't." The pause behind his words had her belly flipping, waiting for the other shoe to drop. "You have my forgiveness, although it isn't necessary. But it's time you forgive yourself."

His words punched straight through her chest. He was right—she'd spent years atoning for her sins; maybe it was time to move past them and let them go instead.

Fourteen

"What are your intentions with my sister?"

Jameson had been waiting for this conversation, but he'd wanted to give Gray and Kinley the space they needed first.

"That's a good question." No, that was a lie. It was a terrible question because Jameson had no idea what the answer was.

"I thought so, too. While you're answering questions, why don't you include an explanation for why you've spent days with my sister, knowing she was in danger the entire time, and only bothered to let me know what was happening when someone tried to *kidnap* her."

Gray's words were level enough, but Jameson could hear the suppressed irritation running beneath them.

"Look, man, I did what I thought was right given Kinley's circumstances and her reluctance to let you anywhere near her. The minute I realized that her life was in serious danger, I came clean."

Gray harrumphed, the sound echoing across the empty water around them. But he didn't say anything else, simply leaned out against the railing and stared down at the rush of water churning beneath the ship.

"There's something between you." This time, it wasn't a question, which meant Jameson didn't really need to answer.

But he did anyway. "Yeah."

"What are you going to do about it?"

Jameson's chest tightened. "What can I do? She's skittish, mistrustful of everyone and more likely to bolt than work through a problem. She's spent years running. She hasn't spent more than three months in one place for twelve years."

"And you've spent years growing the roots that were yanked out from under you."

Jameson's eyebrow rose as he turned to take in his friend. He shouldn't be surprised at Gray's knowledge of Jameson's past, but a part of him was. After all, he was usually the person Gray called on to dig up dirt on people. Who knew the man apparently had skills of his own?

"She's also pretty angry with me right now."

"Maybe, but anger fades."

Jameson shook his head. "Sometimes." But given Kinley's difficulty trusting people, he wasn't certain she'd be able to forgive him and move past all the dishonesty and doubt between them.

Before he could voice his concerns, Kinley's devastated voice cut through the quiet. "It's gone."

Rushing onto the deck, she held out the twisted metal that used to nestle in the valley of her breasts. "Gone. Everything's gone."

Crap. He'd meant to talk to her about that this morning, but with Gray showing up hours before expected, it had gotten lost.

"No, it isn't."

Crossing the deck, Jameson dug into the pocket of his shorts and pulled out the unassuming drive he'd placed there. "I made a copy of the files before we left for the ball. I have everything backed up."

"You have everything backed up?" Relief washed across Kinley's features. Followed closely by confusion, anger and betrayal.

Snatching it from his hand, she asked, "When did you copy my drive? I've been wearing it around my neck nonstop since I left for Tampa."

"I copied it while you were sleeping."

Twisting out of his hold, she took several giant steps back. "You mean, after we had sex, while I was asleep and vulnerable, you stole my flash drive and copied the files."

Jameson's chest tightened with dread. "It sounds awful when you put it like that. I knew the information was important and I wanted to make sure we had a copy."

Thunder rolled through her bright blue eyes, turning them into a scary summer storm. "And you didn't think to *ask* me?"

"Oh, I did, but I knew you wouldn't agree. Hell, until two days ago you didn't trust me enough to even tell me what you'd been working on and why someone would want to steal from you and threaten you."

Exasperation flagged her cheeks with bright red. "Because *you* were the one who stole from me."

"Just like you were the one who sneaked out of my bed—after using sex to try to manipulate me—to skulk around my ship and break into my server room."

"I didn't break into anything. And only because you wouldn't let me near a computer."

At some point they'd both taken steps forward until the space between them disappeared. Kinley's bare feet kissed the toe of his deck shoes. Her hands balled into tight fists on her hips and her chest rose and fell with the force of her words and her anger.

Jameson paused, trying to decide between kissing the hell out of her and strangling her. Purposely bringing his voice down, he modulated each word as he said, "I did what needed to be done. I was trying to help and protect you."

"I didn't ask for your help or your protection."

His own hands curled into ineffectual fists. It was either that or reach for her and probably make the situation worse. "Maybe not, but clearly, you need both."

Her mouth thinned and her eyes flashed with pure rage. "Who elected you my savior? At no time during this entire situation have you asked for my opinion or help. In fact, you've frozen me out, lied to me, manipulated me and maneuvered me where you wanted."

Damn, looking back on things from her perspective, he supposed that's exactly what he'd done. "Because you're stubborn, lonely and unwilling to trust anyone. Kinley, Gray and I have been trying to get you to come to us for help for a year. You left me no choice but to maneuver you."

Reaching up, Jameson rubbed at the tightness in his chest. It felt like a block was sitting right there, pressing down on everything inside. For some reason, he felt like he was losing everything all over again. Just like he did when the officer had shown up to tell him that his parents were dead.

How had that happened? How had he let himself fall for a woman he knew would walk away?

"Your life is pure chaos, Kinley. Not because it happens to you, but because that's what you choose. You told me you were lonely. You're lonely because that's what you choose. You said there was no one you trusted with the information—even me. Because you refuse to risk letting someone in who might hurt you."

His words hung in the air. Around them, the only sound was the rushing waves as they broke against the bow of the ship. And then Kinley's long, indrawn breath.

"You're right. I've chosen to isolate myself. Because I've been hurt. Because the people who should have protected me did everything but. And it is a choice. One I can change."

For the briefest moment, the warmth of possibility spread through Jameson's chest, beating back the smothering pressure.

Until Kinley took a huge step around him and approached Gray. Jameson had been so focused on Kinley he'd forgotten his friend was still standing behind him.

Turning, he watched Kinley stop in front of Gray and hold out the flash drive. "I'd like your help."

Kinley stood in the parking lot and tried not to stare at the ship sitting quietly in the early evening light. She shouldn't feel betrayed that he hadn't even come to say goodbye, but she did.

Oh, she was still angry with him, but as hours had passed, her tangled emotions had softened.

He shouldn't have copied her flash drive without her permission. But then she'd done a few things herself that she wasn't proud of, either.

The end result was that Gray had the information he needed to make the people at One Peace pay. Clearly, they were behind the attempted theft of her money, the demand for the return of the funds she'd stolen and the thwarted kidnapping. Rather than chase after the people involved in those crimes—because they were likely paid help—Gray and Stone had decided to cut the head off the snake and hope the body died, too.

So she was on her way to Charleston where they were going to place her in a safe house until the immediate danger was over.

She assumed Jameson was aware of the plan, although he hadn't been involved in any of the discussions. Nor had he been there when the team had remotely reviewed the evidence file that had taken her months to build.

"Are you ready?" Gray's voice broke into her staring match with the ship. Who would have thought the damn thing would come to feel more like home than any place she'd ever been in her life?

Nodding, she slipped into the car. Gray followed to the other side, but the driver didn't immediately leave. The car idled, the engine quiet and waiting.

"You're sure this is what you want to do?"

No, she wasn't. But the pit in her stomach urged her to just go. Leave behind Jameson and the jumbled-up emotions he made her feel. The fear. The hope. The undeniable urge to bury her face in his chest whenever he was near.

Jameson Neally made her vulnerable. So the best thing to do was walk away before she got hurt. Again.

She opened her mouth to say yes, but the single word wouldn't push past her lips.

Reaching across the seat, Gray grabbed her hand and squeezed. "I know for all intents and purposes I've only been your big brother for less than a day, but can I give you some advice?"

A choked laugh scraped against her throat. "You've been my big brother all my life… I just acknowledged it. And I think you have plenty of brotherly advice to catch up on, so why not start now?"

"Love is never easy, but that's what makes it worthwhile. There's something about the human psyche that makes us appreciate that which we have to work for. Caring about someone, trusting someone, is never easy. But in my experience, it's usually worth it."

Kinley just shook her head. "How can you say that? So many people have betrayed you, used you."

He shrugged, wide shoulders rubbing against the tight material of his shirt. "Maybe, but not by the ones who truly mattered."

Shifting, Gray moved so he could better look at her. "You've spent a long time running. And for good reason. But now's the time to ask yourself what you really want and whether running is the best way to get it. You aren't alone anymore, Kinley, and I'm not just talking about me."

Kinley sagged against the plush seat. Jameson, that's what she wanted. The answer was simple and quick. A life with him.

Having someone in her life…it was never a dream she allowed herself to have. But somehow, he found a way to sneak in under her defenses. To tempt her with the reality of something so sweet, yet so out of her reach.

Jameson was right. She'd fought him and herself, putting up barriers every chance she got. Oh, he'd made plenty of mistakes, but every time he'd manipulated and lied to her, he'd had her best interests at heart. That didn't make it right, but maybe that made it something they could work on. Didn't she owe it to herself to find out?

As if reading her mind, Gray's quiet words slipped through the last of her defenses. "Self-preservation is a hard lesson to turn off. Especially when it's been as ingrained as it has been for you and me."

Such a true statement.

But the punches kept coming. "I'm pretty sure, the little I know about Joker's background, he's learned some of those lessons. The hard way."

The details Jameson had shared with her about his past flooded through her. The story of his parents' deaths. The friend and mentor who had betrayed him. Jameson had plenty of reasons for his own walls to be high…and yet he'd dropped them. With her.

Squeezing her eyes shut, Kinley breathed, "Dammit."

Beside her, Gray chuckled. Reaching across her, he opened the door. "I always knew you were smart."

Jameson stood on the deck, watching as Gray held the door open and Kinley slipped inside.

She was truly gone.

Turning away, he headed into the belly of the ship. He'd given the staff the night off, insisted they take the opportunity to enjoy New Orleans. Even Eric had gone ashore, which meant it was just him and the *Queen*.

As it should be.

With no destination in mind, he wandered slowly through the ship. No, that wasn't true. He knew exactly where he was headed—her stateroom—so purposely veered in the opposite direction.

But everywhere he turned, the ghost of her remained. Even at the stern of the ship, by the Jet Skis.

He couldn't stop the sad smile at the memory of her laughter and happiness as she flew across the water at top speed.

Sliding his hands into the pockets of his shorts, Jameson leaned against the side of the ship and simply stared out across the horizon. The harbor behind him, the stretch of open water should have tempted him, but it didn't.

Silence pressed against him, broken only by the ding of an email dropping into his inbox.

Pulling the phone from his pocket, he realized the email wasn't from his account, but from Kinley's account that he'd cloned days ago.

Curiosity had him clicking it open, but the minute he did, Jameson jerked straight. The email was a picture of the *Queen* sitting in the New Orleans harbor. It had to have been taken only a few minutes ago because the front end of the car Kinley had just left in was visible in the far corner.

As creepy as that was, the words beneath the picture were worse.

I told you what would happen. Tick, tick, boom.

Without thought, Jameson ran to the platform at the stern of the ship and dived off. Warm water engulfed him. Kicking hard, he swam as far away as he could before resurfacing.

Bobbing out in the middle of the harbor, he turned

to look at the *Queen*. Nothing. The quiet silhouette of the ship stood against the gray gloom of early night.

He was starting to feel silly for diving off.

And then the world exploded.

Fifteen

The sound hit her first, nearly forcing her double from the impact of the wave. Heat rolled over her next, even as her body was flung against the hard pavement.

Not from the blast, but from Gray dropping on top of her.

Kinley's ears rang and her head felt fuzzy. The world went wonky for several seconds, everything fading away, before it all snapped back into unbelievable focus.

Something had exploded. Pushing up from the ground, she stared at the *Queen*, horror rolling through her. "Jameson."

Kinley heard the anguish in her own voice.

Without thought, she raced across the parking lot.

Smoke rolled up from the shell of the ship. Flames licked against the darkening sky.

Guilt and bile rolled through her belly and up her throat. If he was dead, it would be her fault.

"Jameson. Jameson." She barely recognized her own voice as she raced up the gangway. Strong hands snatched her from behind, hauling her to a stop.

"You can't go on board, Kinley. It isn't safe."

She fought against her brother with everything she had. "Let me go. He needs me."

But Gray's hold only tightened. His arms became bands around her waist, holding her up off the ground so that her feet couldn't find purchase.

Around her, there was chaos. Sirens wailed in the distance. People gathered to watch. All while her world was falling apart in front of her.

Until that moment, she hadn't realized just how much Jameson meant to her.

"Hey, someone get help." The shout sounded from farther down the marina. A spurt of hope shot through Kinley's system. This time when she pushed against Gray's hold, his arms loosened.

In the darkness, she watched as a tall, wet figure was hauled up out of the water and onto the pavement. The light was too dim, so she couldn't be sure, but the flutter in her belly knew.

The figure flopped onto the ground, rolling onto his back. The hacking sound of coughing cut through the air. A terrible, precious sound.

"I'm fine." The words came out as a wheeze, but Kinley would recognize that voice anywhere.

Sliding to her knees beside him, she let her hands run over every inch of Jameson's body. "Where are you hurt?"

Grasping her hands, he brought them to his chest and held them. "Nowhere. I was already in the water and just had the wind knocked out of me by the blast."

"You were in the water? What were you doing in the water?"

Jameson shook his head and let his gaze move pointedly around the gathering crowd.

Before she could make a move, Gray was there. He swooped in, made sure Jameson could walk and practically before she could blink all three of them were in the car, heading away from the marina.

"Wait." Kinley turned to look at the melee behind her and, through the flashing lights of the emergency vehicles congregating at the scene, got a clear view of the carnage.

The *Queen of Hearts*, Jameson's pride and joy, was destroyed. Honestly, she was surprised it still floated, but that might not be the case for very long. A huge hole gaped in the side of the ship and the top several decks were unrecognizable.

The yacht and everything onboard were destroyed.

"Don't we need to speak to the authorities or something?"

"No." Twisting from the passenger seat to look at her, Gray's words left no room for argument. "Now is the time to get you both to safety. Jameson, you told me the staff had the night off. Was anyone else on board?"

"No. They'd already left."

"How did you get off in time?"

Her brother asked the question that had been spinning through her mind.

"I cloned Kinley's phone days ago. She got an email with a picture of the *Queen* and a few words that made me think there was a bomb on board. Luckily, I was already at the stern and jumped. Just in time."

Kinley stared at Jameson, her brain spinning on what he was telling her. Reaching into her bag, she pulled out the phone she'd finally gotten back, opened it and stared at the email she hadn't seen. Horror rushed through her. She knew she should probably be upset that he'd cloned her phone, but considering it had saved his life, she couldn't seem to muster up the emotion.

"I thought you were dead," she breathed out.

His lips quirked up into a lopsided grin. "I'm not. But it's nice to know that would have upset you."

"Upset me? Jameson, I couldn't breathe when I thought you were hurt or worse. I was ready to run onto that burning ship to find you. The only reason I didn't was because Gray wouldn't let me."

"I don't know what to say to that." His pale green eyes blinked, and slow words followed. "No, that's not true. Kinley, watching you walk away tonight nearly gutted me. I've only felt that level of devastation once in my life, when I found out my parents had died. That night, I felt utterly alone. And I've felt that way for a very long time. Until you."

His words distorted with emotion, but he kept

going. "I know I went about things all wrong, and if I had it to do over again, I would change so much. I would take that first step in trusting you because I knew you couldn't. I'd ask your permission to copy your drive, call in your brother, or sequester you in the middle of the Gulf. I would have included you instead of making decisions for you."

The echo of panic that had filled every inch of her throbbed inside her chest, but next to that emotion was something much stronger.

"I love you." The words were a shock, out of her mouth before they'd really been a thought. But once they were out, she realized she never wanted to take them back. "I love you."

"I'm sorry." He reached for her, pulling her against his body so that he could simply feel her. "What you want and need matters to me, Kinley. I'm sorry for lying to you, manipulating you and pushing you into a corner. I'm sorry for doing exactly what your parents did by taking your choices away from you. And I promise, if you give me another chance, I'll never exclude you in that way again.

"Your happiness is what matters most to me. If you want to be a gypsy, moving every few months, so that we can save the world from one nasty criminal at a time, I'll be right beside you."

His arms tightened around her, pulling her close. Kinley felt a shiver rock his body. "Bobbing in the water, staring up at the Queen as smoke poured out the gaping hole in her side, one thing became very clear to me. For years I thought of that ship as my home. I expected to feel this huge sense of loss when I realized she was gone. But I didn't. Losing you was a hell of a lot more devastating. Home isn't about where you live, it's about the people you share your life with."

With a sigh of hope, Kinley reached for him. "I'm sorry, too. I need to trust and let people in. Not just you, but others as well. I don't have to be alone anymore." No, it was more than that. "I don't want to be alone anymore."

Looking straight into her eyes, he said, "I'll be honest, your life scares me. I lost the two people I cared about most and it sent my life into turmoil. Chaos that it took me a long time to get out of. The thought of you being hurt…" His hold on her tightened. "What you do is dangerous. But being without you scares me more and I'm willing to do whatever it takes to be part of your life."

Setting her palm against his face, Kinley leaned closer, welcoming the melting heat from his body. "I'm tired of the life I've been leading. Help me find another way. A way to do good and give back without sacrificing my safety. Or losing you."

Jameson wrapped a hand around the nape of her neck, urging her closer even as he kept an inch of distance between them. "You fascinate me, Kinley. You frustrate and challenge me. This need for you drives me crazy and makes me whole. I never want to take your choices away, but God, when this is over, I want you to stay. For you, for me, for us."

Kinley leaned forward, pressing her forehead

against his. "I was so mad when I realized you'd copied that drive, not because it really mattered, but because for the first time in years I trusted someone and it felt like a betrayal, one that cut deep."

Jameson's hand on her nape squeezed. "I'm sorry," he whispered. "That wasn't my intention."

"I know that. I knew it then. You're important to me, Jameson. More than I expected or was looking for, and I want to follow this path. There are a few things we need to figure out, but I want to do that. With you."

Jameson's mouth met hers. She opened, letting him in without a moment of hesitation. There were no games or agendas, not anymore. Just connection, understanding and heat.

Kinley wasn't sure how long they kissed, light and shadow glinting as the car raced toward the airport. All she knew was that in that moment, she never wanted him to let her go.

But the loud sound of Gray's voice interrupted them.

"As touching as this moment is, we do have a few loose ends to tie up."

Epilogue

Kinley stared at the image of Meredith Mercado—a well known journalist who apparently had ties to Stone Surveillance through her husband, although the details of the connection were still a little fuzzy—as she outlined the facts uncovering a high-profile corruption scandal at one of the world's most influential charitable organizations.

Her voice continued as the split screen moved to footage of powerful people from all over the world being led out of office buildings, houses and estates in handcuffs. Business moguls, high-ranking politicians and power brokers.

Stone and Gray had uncovered the source of the threats against her- a high ranking politician from France who had been a source for some of the information Kinley had gathered. He'd hired local thugs to carry out his orders. All of them had been quietly rounded up and charged with their crimes. The politician had been part of the One Peace arrests.

Kinley should feel satisfaction. And she did. But there was also a tiny part of her that was a little sad because watching the footage meant the last vestiges of her previous life were gone.

From across the room, Kinley watched her brother give an interview to a New Orleans news station.

"My family is devastated by the loss of my sister and a good friend in the explosion at the marina. Preliminary reports suggest it was an engine malfunction and a freak accident. The yacht had reportedly experienced engine failure out to sea just days before. At this time we request your respect so that both families can grieve in private."

It didn't faze her that the entire story was fabricated. Apparently, Stone Surveillance had the resources to ensure no one would contradict the story being told. After much discussion, the team had decided it was in everyone's best interests to let the world think she and Joker were dead. That way, even after the multiple arrests, if anyone from One Peace was left to pick up the pieces Kinley and Jameson would no longer be on their radar.

Jameson slipped behind her, wrapping his arms around her waist. "You ready for this?"

Her belly fluttered, anticipation and a little apprehension. The unknown was always scary, but this time when she disappeared, she wasn't doing it alone. And it would be the last time she ever had to run.

Rolling her head, Kinley placed a quick kiss on the underside of Jameson's jaw. "Absolutely, but I am a little disappointed we never could recover the fifty million."

"Not that we particularly need it," Jameson mused.

"Maybe not, but it's a mystery left unsolved. And that's a lot of money. I don't like the idea of it being in the hands of anyone from One Peace."

Disengaging the mic from his lapel, Gray moved out from in front of the small camera the tech crew had set up for his feed to New Orleans.

"We're clear," the tech said.

Heading for the far door, Gray paused. She expected him to issue some reminder about the protocol they had in place for protecting their new identities. But neither was prepared when he said, "By the way, *I* have Kinley's money," before walking away.

Jameson turned to Kinley, "What did he just say?"

"I'm pretty sure he just said that he has my money. But that makes no sense." Kinley stared after her brother. "Does it?"

Jameson's voice was slow and deliberate, thoughts filtering through to words. "I wouldn't think Gray had the skills to do something like that, but then I wasn't exactly being careful or stealthy when I moved the money.

"But he did break into my phone and change the ringtone for his calls. And now that I think about it, there have been a few times he provided some information that might not have been readily available through normal channels."

Jameson stared at her, eyes wide. "Son of a bitch."

"So, it was coincidence?"

"No, someone was actively in the process of stealing your money when I took it. Gray was probably keeping an eye on both of us. The money didn't disappear until a day after I took it, though. And not until after Gray called me that morning, asking questions that seemed innocent at the time."

Kinley laughed, a small sound that continued to grow until she was doubled over, arms wrapped around her belly and tears streaming down her face.

"This isn't funny."

Finally, wiping away stray tears, she stood upright. "Oh, it really is. He bested both of us."

Okay, she had a point. One his ego wasn't ready to concede.

Shaking his head, Jameson pulled her into his arms. "You could still change your mind about all this."

It was the easiest thing to shake her head. "No, I want to do this. With you."

"Thank God," he whispered, "because I wouldn't be able to let you go."

She and Jameson both had agreed to give up their former lives. It had been a little easier for her than for him, as he'd spent years building a life and reputation as a hacker. But in the end, he'd decided to take the leap with her.

Although it wasn't like they were leaping far.

Anderson Stone had provided them both with new identities and because neither of them had been tied directly to Stone Surveillance before—Joker had always interacted with the team remotely except for Stone and Gray—they were going to settle right there in Charleston.

It offered Kinley the chance to build a relationship with her brother and them both the opportunity to take permanent positions with Stone Surveillance. They could continue their work, as allies instead of adversaries, and benefit so many people who needed help.

They'd talked about it and Kinley realized that was as important to Jameson as it was to her.

The future would be much different than she'd ever expected. But whatever happened, she and Jameson were going to figure it out together.

Gray pushed back into the conference room, a smile curling his stern lips. "Ready to meet the team?"

"Let's do this," Jameson whispered as he placed a soft kiss onto her lips.

With a nod, Kinley grasped his hand and together, they walked into whatever the future might hold.

* * * * *

HARLEQUIN
PLUS

Try the best multimedia subscription service for romance readers like you!

Read, Watch and Play.

Experience the easiest way to get the romance content you crave.

Start your **FREE TRIAL** at
www.harlequinplus.com/freetrial.